TWIST MY CHARM

The Popularity Spell

TWIST MY CHARM

The Popularity Spell

TONI GALLAGHER

Random House  New York

Text copyright © 2015 by Toni Gallagher
Jacket art copyright © 2015 by Helen Huang

All rights reserved. Published in the United States by
Random House Children's Books, a division of Penguin Random House LLC, New York.

Random House and the colophon are registered trademarks of Penguin Random House LLC.

Visit us on the Web! randomhousekids.com

Educators and librarians, for a variety of teaching tools,
visit us at RHTeachersLibrarians.com

Library of Congress Cataloging-in-Publication Data
Gallagher, Toni.
Twist my charm / Toni Gallagher.—First edition.
p. cm.—(Twist my charm)
Summary: Eleven-year-old Cleo is having trouble fitting in at her private school
in Los Angeles, but when she and her friend Sam try to improve things using the
voodoo doll her uncle Arnie sent, there are unexpected results.
ISBN 978-0-553-51115-4 (trade)—ISBN 978-0-553-51116-1 (lib. bdg.)—
ISBN 978-0-553-51117-8 (ebook)
[1. Interpersonal relations—Fiction. 2. Vodou—Fiction. 3. Middle schools—Fiction.
4. Schools—Fiction. 5. Single-parent families—Fiction. 6. Theater—Fiction.
7. Los Angeles (Calif.)—Fiction.] I. Title.
PZ7.G355Twi 2015 [Fic]—dc23 2014022807

Printed in the United States of America
10 9 8 7 6 5 4 3 2 1
First Edition

To Con and Taps.
You knew I could do it . . . I think.

The Popularity Spell

A masterpiece! That's what this drawing is going to be. It's an intergalactic panda shooting rainbows out of his butt, and one day people will look at it in an art gallery and talk in whispers about how the artist, Cleo Margaret Nelson, was only eleven years old at the time, but had the talent of somebody really rich and famous.

All the picture needs is a little more yellow to fill in the stars and maybe some blue for Pandaroo's eyes, and then my masterpiece will be complete. Pandaroo is just one of the characters I've created as an aspiring animator, and one day I want them all to be in cartoons on TV and big-time movies, not just on pieces of paper.

I search in my desk and find some colored pencils poking out between the homework papers, candy wrappers, and other junk. That's when I hear someone say my name from the front of the classroom.

It's Kevin, my teacher. "Cleo, didn't you bring a snack for break?"

This is bad for a couple of reasons.

First of all, I have a teacher named Kevin. That's just weird. Back in Ohio, teachers were named Mr. Nagurny or Mrs. Stem, like normal adults with last names, not Kevin or Janet or Roberta, like they're your friends. But I've lived in Los Angeles for three months now, and like they say here, *whatever!*

Second of all, this school's snack break is only fifteen minutes long and you're supposed to bring something "delicious and nutritious" to eat while you sit at your desk doing tasks that are "enriching to your life and spirit," whatever that means.

On top of all that, no, I do not have a snack for snack break. But I don't want Kevin bringing attention to it in front of everybody. Especially Madison Paddington.

Madison Paddington—Maddy Paddy to her friends—is eleven like me, but she's a *Los Angeles* eleven, which is more like fourteen anywhere else in the world. Her hair is like golden sunlight on a wheat field in a painting you'd see in a museum. Her jeans probably cost three hundred dollars. And her teeth are totally straight and shiny; she'll never need braces.

Then there's me. I've got a gap between my front teeth, and Dad says I'm going to need dental work "out the wazoo."

"It's okay," I say to Kevin. "My dad forgot to pack my snack." And I forgot to check, but I don't tell him that.

"Her dad packs her lunch?" Madison whispers to her friends Kylie Mae and Lisa Lee. "What a baby."

Kevin doesn't hear her, though, because he's busy asking loudly, "Kids, does anyone have a snack they can share with Cleo?" His question makes everyone look at me, which is the last thing I want—ever!

"I'm not hungry," I say quietly, but it's too late. Someone's hand has shot up in the air.

It's Scabby Larry, the kid nobody likes. He's so excited, it's like someone asked him if he wanted peanut M&M's and a free unicorn ride, not to share his snack. "I've got carrot sticks! Come on over," he says, holding up his plastic baggie and smiling way too big.

"I'm really not hungry." I look at Kevin and hope he'll just let me sit at my desk and enrich my life and spirit without a delicious, nutritious snack.

"Part of the experience here at Friendship Community School, Cleo, is about sharing and companionship. Enjoy some of Larry's carrots." So I have no choice.

The room is completely quiet as I stand up from my desk. My chair screeches against the ground, sounding like an injured coyote. It feels like it takes forever to walk across the room. No matter how many steps I take, Scabby Larry's desk looks farther and farther away. Why did *he* have to be the one who raised his hand?

I bet everybody is staring at my non-name-brand sneakers and my pants that are too high above my ankles now that I've had a growth spurt. I thought my clothes were fine before we moved to LA, but now I think about what's wrong with them all the time.

Then I make the world's biggest mistake.

I take the whole bag from Scabby Larry's hand.

"Oh, I meant take *some*," he says, pulling back the baggie and handing me a few carrots.

The laughs in the room are like Fourth of July fireworks—one or two quiet ones at first, followed by a big explosion. Madison giggles and says, "They must eat like piggies in Ohio." Then her friends make some piglike grunts. But they're quiet enough that Kevin doesn't hear them.

I go back to my desk and sit. I can tell everyone is watching me eat this handful of carrot sticks that rightfully belongs inside Scabby Larry's stomach. And even though I know I shouldn't, I look over at Madison. She pretends like she's eating carrots in a big exaggerated way, licking her perfectly puffy lips with their glittery pink gloss. Then she puts her pinkie out, all dainty and casual, and pushes her nose up like a pig's.

I hate her.

Okay, Dad doesn't like it when I use the word *hate,* so I'm supposed to say I really *don't like* Madison. Neither does Samantha, who is looking at me with a sad frowny face.

Samantha is one of my friends at my new school. To be honest, she's my only friend, but I hate—I mean, *don't like*—saying it that way because it makes me sound seriously lame.

Samantha has known Madison and the others all her life, but she's nothing like them. The funny thing is, she's nothing like me either. I'm too tall and too skinny and my hair is a muddy yellow tangled mess. Sam is shorter and built like a pug (a cute one) with a mop of frizzy black hair. If we got into a fight, I bet she could steamroll me with her puggy body and I'd only have a pair of bony elbows to defend myself with.

Luckily we don't fight, though, because we're best friends.

I keep eating the carrots. Every time I swallow it feels like sharp edges are scraping my throat. Usually I like carrots just fine but today they taste like dog poop rolled in sawdust and painted orange. Across the room, Scabby Larry is grinning like he did me a big favor.

Kevin finally tells us to put our snacks away because it's time for science. Some of the kids groan, but I don't. I like science most of the time. You get to pour things into beakers and see if they explode and you get to learn about animals—I heard that next year we get to poke around the insides of a frog! Girls like Madison Paddington think that stuff is gross, but I love it.

Sam loves it too. She's super smart and fun and likes almost all the same stuff I do. We became friends my first week of school when I saw her sitting by herself in the lunchroom writing a book about the skunk population of California. I told her I'd draw pictures for it if anyone ever buys it to put in bookstores or on the Internet.

"Today I want to talk about a project that you'll all find

5

really fun," Kevin says. There are more groans in the room because when teachers think things are fun, they almost never are. "In two weeks everyone is going to do a presentation. It's going to count as one-quarter of your grade. Who knows how much one-quarter is?"

I know, but I'm not going to say because it's not math class and I don't need to bring any more attention to myself. Sam knows too, for sure, but she doesn't say anything either.

"Twenty-five percent!" shouts Scabby Larry. Of course *he'd* say it.

"Thank you, Larry," says Kevin. "Yes, twenty-five percent of your grade. Now, before I hear any complaints, here's the fun thing. You get to pick the topic. It can be anything science-related. Animals, vegetables, minerals, technology, inventors. You can do a speech, make a movie, show examples, create a collage. Heck, write a poem if you want to, as long as there's plenty of information in it. . . ."

This *does* sound fun! I stop listening because my mind is already going every which way with all the interesting things I could study. This is not a good thing because I probably should be concentrating on social studies and math and English and the other subjects we learn about the rest of the day. But by the time my dad picks me up in the parking lot after school, I've almost forgotten about the thing that happened with Kevin and Scabby Larry and Madison and the carrots.

Almost.

2

Back home after school, I tell Dad he forgot to pack my snack, and he says exactly what I expect. "You can always pack your own lunch then."

"No, that's okay," I say right away. "You make the best turkey, lettuce, and butter sandwiches in the universe. I could never make them as delicious as you do."

Dad laughs and says that flattery will get me everywhere, whatever that means. And I'm happy I won't have to pack my own lunches when I have much more important things going on, like my science project!

Dad seems excited about it too. He's a website designer so there are lots of computers in our dining room, and he brings one of his laptops into my bedroom while I look online on my own computer. Toby, our Irish setter, sits at our feet with his tongue hanging out. He's got the cutest, furriest face and the worst breath in the world, but I don't care because I love him.

One of Dad's brilliant ideas is for me to write a musical about the inner life of the Costa Rican three-toed sloth. He's being a dork as usual, but I *do* like the idea of picking an animal nobody else would choose. Dad and I find a lot of odd creatures online, like an insect called a walking stick that actually looks like a stick and a hilarious-looking bird called a blue-footed booby, which I'm sure I couldn't say in front of the class without being embarrassed.

Then I find African millipedes, and they look pretty cool! They're sort of like worms, but bigger and more exotic. They're dark and shiny and pudgy, and some can be over ten inches long. They have anywhere from thirty-six to four hundred legs, though it seems like a thousand! I like that they look totally slimy but also weirdly adorable. And according to one website about millipedes, they're not too hard for a kid to take care of. Dad agrees to buy me one at the pet store Pets! Pets! Pets!, so I can live with it, learn about it, and take it to class. I wonder how Madison Paddington will feel when I do my presentation and I hold up the longest, fattest millipede with its millions of little brown legs and its slimy-looking skin as it squirms between my fingers.

I hope she *hates* it.

From the end of our hallway, I hear the doorbell ring.

Toby doesn't run or bark; he just looks up at me and Dad, wondering who's going to answer it. I'm enjoying my millipede research, so I stay put. Dad looks at us both. "Don't bother yourselves," he says, kind of like a joke. "I'll get it."

Dad answers the door and I can hear him talking to a guy, but I can't tell what they're saying. A minute later, Dad yells down the hall, "Cleo! There's a package for you!"

Wow. That's something I've never heard before. I haven't ever gotten a package, and that's how I know it's a major event. Important people get things delivered to their door, not eleven-year-olds like me. It's not like I'm a famous artist . . . yet.

Toby barks and jumps around, almost as happy as I am. We both tear down the hall, his smooth red fur and my messy yellow hair flying, and find Dad standing in the doorway. He's holding something about the size of a shoebox and wrapped in light-brown paper. I grab it from his hands, sit right down in the middle of the floor, and rip it open.

Inside the box is a bunch of crumpled newspaper. I throw that to the ground and finally get to the good stuff. What I find is a little bit . . . weird. But cool. But strange. Lying in the bottom of the box is a rag doll, but not like any rag doll I've ever seen before.

The tan material feels scratchy against my hands, and the filling isn't soft and cuddly like a teddy bear; it's hard like corn kernels or birdseed. The edges of the doll are sewn together with thick brown yarn, and the same kind of yarn is on the doll's head, sticking out at different angles like my dad's does in the morning. Its button eyes are scratched and chipped, and the doll isn't wearing any clothes except a pink tutu around its middle, which looks majorly out of place. There's also a pin with a little black ball on top poked into its shoulder area. That's it.

I hold it up for Dad to see, and he sighs. "Oh jeez. I only know one person who would send you a voodoo doll."

Ohhhh, it's a *voodoo doll*! I think I read a story about those one time. They're for putting charms and hexes on people you don't like. You poke the pin into a part of the doll where you want the bad thing to happen, and then it does. Spooky!

"Who sent it?" I ask Dad. "Do you know?"

"You'll see," he says. "Is there a note or anything?" I put down the doll and look. Inside the box, sort of lining the bottom, is one piece of white paper. It's hard to pull it out with my uneven, bitten nails, but I finally do. The writing is definitely not from a computer or even a typewriter; it looks like it was handwritten by a crazy person or wacky cartoonist. It turns out to be the instructions.

MEET POSITIVE HAPPY VOODOO DOLL—THE VOODOO DOLL WHO WILL MAKE YOUR LIFE BETTER!

Use these simple instructions to achieve your desired effect.

1. A voodoo doll is not a toy. Even when you have good intentions, it is serious business. Use it wisely for the good of others—and yourself!

2. Obtain a strand of hair from the person you would like to hex with positive juju, mojo, gris-gris, hoodoo, or whatever you want to call it. Place said hair atop your new voodoo doll. Positive happy voodoo charms must be performed with a friend to achieve the desired results. The power of two is much stronger than the power of one!

3. Place your pin into the doll where you would like the magic to occur (e.g., top of head for more luxurious hair, wrist for better tennis playing, foot for impressive dance moves). If your hex is more general, put the pin any old place!

4. Concentrate on the intended person and result for at least five minutes.

5. Sit back, relax, and wait for your hex to take effect.

For a second I sit and stare at the scribbled instructions. *Juju, mojo, gris-gris,* and *hoodoo* are words I've never even heard before. They sure sound interesting . . . but there's no way this voodoo doll can be real. It's probably something to play with, a joke. I mean, it'd be cool if it actually worked, but the idea of putting charms and hexes on people sounds like it was made up by some old-time writer of horror stories.

But what if it *is* real? Then what could happen? I reread the instructions, and I quickly realize that while getting a lock of hair from someone wouldn't be easy, step four would be the hardest part. *Concentrate on the intended person and result for at least five minutes.* Me—I can't concentrate on anything for very long. I guess this is a big problem in life, and it's part of the reason I'm at this goofy school where we call teachers by their first name. Friendship Community is a private school (which means it costs money), and it has a class called Focus! (exclamation point and all), where a teacher named Roberta helps some of us kids set goals and get things done and, yes, focus better. The kids who are in it—like me and Samantha and Scabby Larry—have to leave Kevin's classroom twice a week to go to another room across the courtyard, and everybody sees us go. Sometimes I hear kids say it's for slow people and dummies, but Dad says they'll all be working for me one day. I like that idea. And best of all, I wouldn't let Madison and her friends work for me in my fun, fantastic animation factory—ever!

"Did you find a card yet?" Dad asks, which makes me

stop thinking about Focus! and instructions and my future factory. I look around in the crumpled newspaper and find a piece of scrap paper with a couple of sloppy drawings of smiley faces and the words "Happy 11th Birthday, Cleo! Love & magic, from your good ol' Uncle Arnie."

So that's how Dad knew who it was from! Uncle Arnie is his brother—and he's definitely the kind of person who would send a birthday gift seven months late. Dad says they're complete opposites, but not in a good way like me and Sam are.

If I could have a brother or sister, I'd want a sister, and I'd want her to be exactly like Sam. And when we grew up, we'd live in the same house or nearby, or at least talk to each other every single day. Dad only talks with Uncle Arnie on the computer every month or two. They like each other okay, but they're not super close like brothers or sisters should be.

I guess that's why I usually just wave to Uncle Arnie from the background when he's on a video call with Dad. Dad has made him sound like kind of a weirdo, and the stories he writes in his emails and old-fashioned letters are sometimes bizarre. He lives in the state he pronounces "Looooosiana," in an area called the bayou. It's full of creepy dark alleys and mysterious strangers who know all about things like voodoo—and probably juju, hoodoo, and gris-gris too. They cast spells and do bad things to people without even touching them.

Uncle Arnie said someone had done that to him years ago, and that's why he has a big icky burn across the inside of his right hand. He said that even though no one was around, an "unseen force" pushed his hand onto the burner of his stove. Dad laughed when he heard that, and told me there were lots of other ways Uncle Arnie could have burned his hand. Maybe he tripped or something . . . but maybe it *was* a voodoo spell. Who can say?

Dad walks toward his dining room office, rolling his eyes and pulling at his black-and-gray hair. "Your uncle," he says. "What a goofball. He *would* think that was a smart gift for an eleven-year-old."

"What's wrong with it?" I ask.

"Oh, nothing, it's only a toy. But a slightly inappropriate one."

"Why is it inappropriate?"

"Well, Cleo," Dad says kind of seriously, "your uncle Arnie is . . . an unusual person and he gets mixed up in things that get him into trouble."

"Like his hand!" I say, excited to have an example.

"Kind of. Let's just say he's a free spirit who doesn't pay a lot of attention to the real world around him. And he believes in dopey things like voodoo."

"So you don't believe in it?"

"Cleo," Dad says, making a face like I should know better. "There's nothing real about voodoo. It's a bunch of weird, ghoulish stories that some people tell—people who don't have anything better to do with their lives. I don't want you wasting too much time with it."

"What about juju and hoodoo and mojo?"

"I'm sure it's all the same thing, Cleo. Pure silliness."

I don't tell Dad about the instructions, how this doll isn't bad and scary, and how it can be used for good things. He still won't like it. So I nod like I'm listening carefully and seriously. But inside I'm glad I got an "inappropriate" present seven months after my birthday. And I think Sam is going to like it too!

3

In the morning, I rush around to get ready like I do every day. Dad tells me to pick out my clothes the night before, but how can I decide on Thursday night what color I want to wear on Friday? Today I still don't know, so I put on a shirt with all different kinds of colorful stripes. And though I swear I always leave my sneakers on the floor right where I take them off, they're never in the same place in the morning. Sometimes I blame it on Toby, but today I find one sneaker on my dresser in front of my new voodoo doll. That's pretty strange. I'm not saying I think the voodoo doll moved it. But what if he did?

No, that's crazy. I'm sure I did and forgot.

"Hurry up, Cleo! Time to go!" Dad shouts, so I run down the hall past him and out the front door. I'm halfway to his car when he asks, "Forget anything?"

I turn around and he's holding up my recyclable lunch bag.

"Thanks, Dad," I say, walking back and taking it from him. "I hope you didn't forget the snack this time."

"Well, remember, if I make a mistake, *you* can always pack your lunches."

That's the last thing I want, so I just say, "I love you, Dad," and run to the car.

I make it through snack break without any incidents because Dad packed me trail mix. He even included chocolate chips. He was probably sorry he forgot yesterday's snack, so I lucked out with something that is both nutritious *and* delicious!

The day goes okay until it's time for Focus! class. Of course Scabby Larry jumps out of his chair like he's excited to go. "Have fun with your boyfriend Scabby," Madison whispers to me as I get up.

I can't tell what's wrong with Scabby Larry—he looks okay on the outside—but Sam told me that in second grade he got caught picking off one of his scabs and eating it. She said no one talks to him much unless they have to, so I probably shouldn't either. So I don't. It's bad enough to be the new kid who Madison Paddington hates; I don't need anyone to think I like Scabby Larry too.

"He's not my boyfriend," I say, wishing I could come up with something better.

"He's not Cleo's boyfriend because he's *your husband*!" Samantha says as she walks past Madison's desk.

Now *that* was a good one! I have to be more like her!

Samantha's in Focus! class too, which is weird because she has so much focus, it's almost scary. When she gets obsessed with things (like video games, or guitar playing, or baking banana bread), she won't do anything else—including taking a shower or going to sleep or even eating. If it's a class for slow people and dummies, like the "popular" kids claim, Sam definitely does not belong. But she makes the best of it.

As we walk across the courtyard lawn to Focus! class, I tell her that I got a super-cool package in the mail yesterday and she'll have to come over this weekend to see what it is. She begs and begs for me to tell her, but I give her a smirk and say she has to wait.

We get to the Focus! room, where our teacher, Roberta, is putting up one of her famous handmade posters against the blackboard. They say things like BELIEVE IN YOURSELF and REACH FOR YOUR DREAMS. Today's is YOU CAN DO IT!

"You can do what?" Samantha whispers to me. "Pick your nose?"

"Hey, I can do that!" I laugh, and pretend to dig in my nostril. "I can also cross my eyes." We both do that until

Roberta tells everyone to quiet down. We spend the next forty-five minutes doing exercises, like pointing out the differences between two pictures Roberta shows us and playing a game where you turn a card over and try to remember where its match is. I'm sure it's a lot more fun than whatever Madison and Kylie Mae and Lisa Lee are doing. It's actually not a bad way to end the week . . . until I'm waiting for Dad to pick me up in the parking lot after school. Sam is already gone, but Madison is not.

She stands next to me, closer than she needs to be. It's a big sidewalk.

"Did you and Scabby Larry plan your wedding in Focus! class?" she asks.

"We don't plan weddings in Focus! class," I say, immediately realizing that was not the right response.

"Oh, so you're planning your wedding this weekend then."

"No! You are!"

"Are you going to wear that adorable striped shirt on your honeymoon?" she asks. "It looks like something a clown would wear."

What is there to say to that? I shuffle my feet for a second, sticking out my neck to see if Dad's car is pulling in.

It's not.

"Are you named after a clown? Cleo sounds like a clown's name. Cleo the clown."

Oh no. I hope this doesn't become a nickname like "Scabby Larry" did. I just stand there, quiet and shuffling, wishing I could think of smart things to say back like Samantha does.

A second later I see Dad's car. I run toward it before he can get too close. I don't need Madison commenting on how it's not new or fancy or how it could use a wash. I jump in the passenger seat and slam the door. "Let's go," I say.

"Lovely to see you too, Cleo." Dad then tells me that it's dangerous to run in parking lots. He doesn't know how dangerous it is standing on the curb with Madison Paddington!

I promise him I won't do it again. As we drive away, I look back and see Madison standing alone now, looking back and forth. I hope she has to wait all weekend.

When I wake up the next day, the first thing I do is smile because Samantha is coming over! And also because it's Saturday, my favorite day of the week.

Sundays are nice too, but you know you're going to have school the *next* day, and that makes you a little sad and gloomy inside, even when it's sunny and bright, like it is almost every day in California.

Outside my window I can see it's one of those shiny LA days, the kind of day where Dad has already shouted three times for me to take Toby for a walk around the lake across the street.

When Dad said we were moving to Los Angeles, I

thought we'd live near the beach or movie stars or at least some ridiculously rich people. We don't. We live in a normal neighborhood with hills and trees and sidewalks. The only semi-special thing is our lake. Dad always tells me that Mom said lakes were magical places because she met Dad when they worked at a camp on a beautiful lake in a forest. She'd say that there's magic everywhere in life if you know how to look for it. But I lived in Ohio for eleven years and four months and it wasn't so great. I never saw anything special. And I haven't seen anything magical in California either. Unless getting a voodoo doll counts.

I know I'm not supposed to pay too much attention to my new doll because of what Dad said about voodoo, but it's hard not to. His button eyes seem to be staring at me as I sit at my computer. I almost type in something about voodoo, but I force myself to look up millipedes instead. Right as I'm reading that ring-tailed lemurs rub millipedes on themselves as bug repellent, I hear the doorbell ring. Sam is here! I run down the hall, then stop fast so I can slide in my socks on our hardwood floor.

"It's Samanthaaaaaa!" I shout, opening the front door. She's next to her mom, who's dressed up all fancy with her makeup done and her straight black hair pulled back into the kind of ponytails actresses have at awards shows. I notice that she's taller than Dad because he's in sneakers and she's wearing high heels. The shoes look totally uncomfortable, but she definitely looks pretty in them!

"You look nice today, Paige," Dad says. "Got big plans this afternoon?"

"Oh, not really, Bradley. Just some errands. And shopping." She puts her hand on my dad's arm. Her fingernails are perfect and red. "I hope you don't mind watching the two crazy girls for a few hours."

"Of course not. You two go play," Dad says to me and Sam.

"Dad, we're eleven. We don't play. This isn't a playdate." I tell him this all the time. It was okay to "play" when I was a kid, but when I said "playdate" once here, Sam told me it was *not* a cool term for sixth graders at all.

I hear Dad saying "Sorry," but I've already grabbed Sam by the arm and I'm pulling her down the hallway. "So, are you finally gonna show me this birthday present you've been talking about?" she asks.

I stop in front of my closed bedroom door like I'm guarding it. "I don't know. It's pretty amazing."

Samantha grabs for the doorknob, but I throw my body in front of it. "Nope! Not yet," I say. "You're going to have to do something to prove yourself worthy."

"Like what?"

"Hmmm," I think out loud. "How about you . . . kiss Scabby Larry?"

"No way!" she shouts, trying to push me out of the doorway. But I stand strong.

"Okay. You have to put your arm around Madison Paddington and say, 'Mmmm, you smell like tulips.'"

"Not gonna happen!" Samantha says, and this time I let her push me away from the door.

"Okay, where is it?" she asks, her eyes zooming from the floor to the ceiling and to every corner in between.

"Close your eyes and I'll show you."

She looks suspicious but closes her eyes anyway. I tiptoe to my dresser and pick up the doll, feeling his scratchy material against my fingers. I hold him in front of her face and tell her to open her eyes, which immediately get big. "Coooool!" she says.

"Yeah, it's my new voodoo doll," I say real casual, like I have lots of things like voodoo dolls lying around the house.

"Can I touch it?" she asks. I hand her the doll and she studies him carefully. She holds him by his arms and wiggles him like he's dancing in his pink tutu. She lays him in one of her hands like she's weighing him. She squeezes him around the middle. She touches each piece of thick brown yarn on his head. I have a strong feeling she's found something new to focus(!) on.

Sam grunts and makes funny "ooga booga" noises, waving the doll in front of my face. I laugh. "This thing is awesome," she says. "Do you think it works?"

"I don't know," I say. "Dad said it's not real. That it's just a toy and I shouldn't get involved with it."

"Well, if it's just a toy, why can't you get involved with it?"

Hmmm. I never thought of it that way.

"How is it supposed to work?" Sam asks.

Now that's a question I can answer! I run into the living room and grab the instructions off the floor where I left them the day the doll arrived. Then I run back to my room. Samantha has plopped herself on my floor, surrounded by my dirty clothes that should be in the hamper and a half-finished drawing of Pandaroo with a new villain I'm creating, Skunkifer. She's a female skunk with long blond hair like Madison's—and she shoots putrid gases out of her butt, not rainbows.

I hand Sam the voodoo instructions. She reads them super fast and says, "So. What are we going to do?"

"What do you mean?" I ask.

"Well, we've got to try it!"

"I know it sounds fun," I say. "But my dad says I shouldn't."

"But he also said it wasn't real. And if it isn't real, why shouldn't we? Just for fun. I mean, if nothing's going to happen, what's the difference?"

As usual, Samantha has a smart point and I don't know how to argue with it.

And why should I?

4

"Who . . . should we hex?" I get a little nervous even asking the question. The instructions say the voodoo doll is meant for good things, but I bet I'd still get in trouble if Dad found out.

"One of us!" Sam answers. "Our hair is right here. On top of our heads. Easy."

She's right. It could be that easy. "But what would the spell be for?" I wonder.

Sam thinks for a second. "Something good that could happen to me at school on Monday. Nothing too wild so we can test it out."

"Okay," I say. "Something special for you. Like, maybe you don't get called on all day."

"Or I get some kind of treat—something I don't get every day."

"Not getting called on is a treat," I say.

"That's true," Sam says. "But it should be something that I can see or touch or taste or smell. Some kind of fun, awesome surprise."

"Sounds good to me!" I say.

"So are we gonna do it?"

I nod.

"Okay," Sam says, "we'll wish that I get a treat." She leans over and puts her black curls in my face. "Grab a hair!"

I bury my nose in her hair. "Mmmm, it smells like tulips," I joke.

Samantha snorts a laugh without looking up. "Come on, pull it!"

I pick through her hair with both hands like an explorer in the jungle. "Let me find ze perfect hair," I say in an accent like a foreign action hero's. "No, zis one is too long. Zis one is too curly. . . ."

Samantha lifts her head up and pulls a hair out herself, squealing a loud "Ow!"

I can't help but laugh. "You should've waited. I would've been gentle!"

"Sometimes when you want to get something done, you have to do it yourself," she says. "So. Are you ready?"

My stomach tightens up in a ball of scared excitement. But I want to show Sam I'm as adventurous as she is, so I say, "Okay, so we concentrate on something special happening to you. A treat that you can see or touch or taste or smell. For five minutes."

"Let's do it," she says.

We cross our legs and sit facing each other. Sam puts the voodoo doll between us and uses one hand to take the pin out of his shoulder. She puts her other hand lightly on the doll's head, so I put my fingers on his legs.

"Where should we put the pin?" I ask.

"Somewhere in the middle," Sam says. "So it can happen anywhere on my body."

This seems fine to me, so Sam holds the pin above her head. We look at each other with big grins.

This is it. We're really doing a voodoo charm.

Samantha brings down her hand and puts the pin in the doll's stomach. I look at his button eyes, imagining Monday at school and Sam thrilled and happy because something great happened to her.

I look up and see Sam's big head of hair across from me. I smile to myself, thinking about when she pulled her own hair out. Why did she shout when she knew it was about to happen? Sam is so funny. . . .

Uh-oh. I realize I'm not focusing and try to get back to the important subject. Sam . . . school . . . something good we can see or touch or smell . . .

This is never going to work, is it? It can't. How could two girls sitting in a bedroom cause something great and wonderful to happen for one of them? Oh well, at least it will be something to laugh about. We can always say we tried and—who knows?—maybe Sam can write a story about it and I can draw pictures of my characters casting voodoo charms . . .

"That's got to be five minutes!" Samantha says suddenly, and I decide to believe her. I know I should have concentrated harder, but I'm sure it won't matter anyway. It's never going to happen.

But I still have the tiniest hope that maybe it could.

Samantha could probably spend the rest of the day focused on my voodoo doll, but I change the subject by turning on my computer and showing her a millipede website. She isn't as impressed with them as I am. She thinks they're slimy-looking, but I convince her it'll be a great science project. She hasn't decided what hers is going to be, and when I suggest skunks, she groans and says, "Ugh, no! I'm already an expert in those from writing my book. I'm thinking maybe the environment. You know how everybody says Earth is getting hotter and hotter? I could solve that. Or I could build a jet pack so we could fly around the buildings at school instead of walking across the courtyard."

If anyone could do it, Sam could.

Unfortunately her mom comes to pick her up before dinnertime. She's probably been shopping somewhere fashionable like Beverly Hills, a place Dad and I never go because it's too rich and fancy. She flashes her sparkly white teeth when she says goodbye to Dad and tells him not to work too hard.

"See ya Monday," I say to Sam, and I know she can hear the extra dash of anticipation in my voice because she gives me a wink back.

Dad cooks hot dogs and Tater Tots for dinner, and while we're eating he makes a great announcement. He found out that Pets! Pets! Pets! is open until nine p.m., so we can go there tonight!

"When?" I ask, shoving Tater Tots in my mouth one after the other. "When, when, when? Are we going right now? I don't have to eat my hot dog; I'm not so hungry anymore. Or I can eat it when I get home. We don't want the store to close."

"Calm down, Cleo," Dad says, slowly dipping a Tot in the puddle of ketchup on his plate. "It's not even seven o'clock yet. We're going to finish our dinner, then I'm going to wash the dishes and you're going to dry them and put them away, and then we're going to pick up my special friend and go to the store."

Ugh. Dad definitely knows how to kill a moment. "Special friend" is the last thing I want to hear. Because Dad's been dating someone.

Dad has a *girlfriend*.

And I guess that's allowed, because my mom died a long, long time ago when I was so little I never really knew her at all. It's been just the two of us ever since, doing things our own way and having our own kind of fun, and we've never needed some lady in our lives.

Back in Ohio, Dad sometimes had "girls who were friends." Mostly they were fine, and we might go to the zoo together or to a street fair, but he would always say they were "only friends" and "she isn't going to be your mom." And he was being honest, because none of them became a real girlfriend who was around for a long time.

But things seem different here.

Since we moved to California, Dad has been spending a lot of time with Terri—that's the name of this one—and I've never met her. I hear him talk to her on the phone a lot, and sometimes he gets me a babysitter so he can go on dates with her. I'm not a baby so I don't want a babysitter anymore. Plus, I don't like that Dad's off having fun without me—eating at restaurants and seeing movies and who knows what other awesome things?

We finish dinner. He washes the dishes and I start putting them away. "Why am I ready to meet your *special friend* now?" I make my voice sarcastic when I say "special friend," but he doesn't seem to notice it.

"Well, we've lived here a good amount of time now. You're settled in. You're comfortable. You know the neighborhood. You've got Samantha. It feels like the right time for you to make another friend."

"She's supposed to be my *friend*?" I ask. "How old is she?"

Dad laughs. "She's not a kid! She's around my age."

"So I'm supposed to be friends with a *grown-up?*" The only grown-ups I've ever known are parents, teachers, and people who work at stores and stuff. I wouldn't call any of them friends.

"Yes," Dad says. "You're going to have to give it a try."

"But why?" I'm probably whining but I don't care. "She's just a girl-who's-a-friend, right?"

That's when he says the thing I don't want to hear.

"She may be more than that, Cleo."

"What?" I shout.

"Quiet down," Dad says. "Listen. I like Terri a lot and I think you will too. I want to spend more time with her and that means she's going to spend time with *us*. So change your attitude, put your shoes on, and get ready to go."

When Dad tells me to change my attitude, I know I shouldn't argue anymore, so I head to my room but stomp a little harder than usual as I go. Dad doesn't need a girlfriend.

I don't like this—at all.

5

I know I need to put on my sneakers, but I really feel like wearing my blue floppy hat to Pets! Pets! Pets! It's got flowers embroidered on it and it's one of my favorites because there's a picture on my bulletin board of my mom wearing it. But the hat's too tight on my big melon head, so I pull it off and grab one that looks like the head of a sock monkey. It covers my whole face. I look in the mirror through the eyeholes and see myself smile through the mouth hole. The smile looks exactly like my mom's, except in her pictures she didn't have a gap between her teeth.

"Cleo!" Dad yells from down the hall. "It's time to go!"

I still have to put on my sneakers. I find one on my desk but I'm not sure where the other one is. Dad yells again. "Cleo! Come right now or we're not going to the pet store at all!" Luckily I find my other sneaker under my bed. I don't know if I put it there or the voodoo doll did, but I throw it on and run down the hall with my laces untied. Dad frowns as soon as he sees me. "Cleo, you are not wearing a ski mask when you meet Terri."

"But I like it!" I say. "What's the matter? Doesn't she like monkeys?"

"It has nothing to do with monkeys."

"You shouldn't date her if she hates monkeys." I'm making a cute face underneath my mask, but Dad can't tell because he can only see my eyes and mouth, not the whole package.

"Cleo." Dad sounds upset now. "Take it off or no millipede."

I lift off the mask. It makes my hair fly in every direction, but I don't care. I don't care what I look like when I meet Terri, and I don't talk at all on the ride over. When we get there, Dad walks up to the front door of a small house, rings the doorbell, and there she is.

She's got long red hair like Toby—but she's nowhere near as cute as he is. Terri is a grown-up like Dad, but she's wearing jeans and sneakers like a kid would, and she's also wearing a T-shirt with a cartoon monkey on it! She might have liked my monkey hat, but now we'll never know.

Dad walks up to my side of the car and opens the door. "Cleo, this is Terri."

"Hi," she says with a little wave. I mutter "hi" back but Dad says, "How about you say, 'Nice to meet you'?" This is pretty silly because Terri can hear that Dad *told* me to say it, and obviously *I* don't think it's nice to meet her at all. But I say it anyway because I want a millipede. She says it's nice to meet me too, but I don't believe her.

"Cleo, why don't you get in the backseat now?" Dad says.

"Why?" I ask. "I got in the front seat when we got in the car and you didn't tell me to get in the back." I know it'd be easier to do what he says, but this is my seat!

"Yes, but Terri's here now. She gets to sit in the front because she's an adult."

That's true, but I have a better argument. "Right. But I'm your *daughter.*"

"Cleo, this is not up for discussion. The grown-ups sit in front. Now move to the back or no millipede."

Ugh. I can't wait to get this millipede so Dad can stop using it to make me do things I don't want to do. Then he says, "I'm sorry we wasted your time, Terri. We're not going to Pets! Pets! Pets! tonight. I'll call you later."

"Okay!" I don't want to, but I give in, unbuckling the seat belt. I climb out the open door and squish my long legs into the seat behind Dad's.

On the way to Pets! Pets! Pets!, Terri and Dad talk about boring adult things like work and schedules and ways to drive to places. I stare at the back of Terri's head like I'm the voodoo doll with his button eyes, trying to make her nervous. One time she catches me. She turns around and smiles but I only frown back.

I feel a little better when we pull into the parking lot of Pets! Pets! Pets! with its big glowing sign of a cartoon dog and cat. As soon as the car is parked, I jump out and run to the door. Dad shouts, "Be careful!" from way behind me, but I don't need to be careful because I'm already there.

Pets! Pets! Pets! has the best smells in the world, like wood chips for guinea pig cages and barrels of doggie treats and big bags of cat litter. It must be the expensive kind of litter, though, because there's a box of it in the cat cage and there's hardly any smell of cat poop or pee.

"Hi! Welcome to Pets! Pets! Pets!" says a worker in a green apron with a spotty teenage face. "My name is Lyle. What can I help you with this evening?"

"We're looking for a millipede," Dad says. Terri is standing next to him. It's dumb that she needs to be so close. If I were a ring-tailed lemur, I'd rub a millipede on me to keep her at a distance.

"Oh, we've got millipedes!" says Lyle. "They're in the back corner; I'll take you there."

I'm ready to go but Terri taps Dad's arm. "You know, millipedes aren't really my thing. I'm more into soft and cuddly than creepy and crawly. Why don't you guys go with Lyle and I'll check out the cats or something?"

"Sounds good!" I say and follow Lyle happily without looking back.

The millipedes are in the corner of the store with the other animals Terri would call creepy and crawly but that I think are totally cool—the reptiles and insects and arachnids. Lyle shows me and Dad a glass case like a fish tank but with dirt and sticks and some pieces of vegetables inside. At first I don't even notice anything crawling around. But then a pudgy head pokes out from some grass, with two little antennae bobbing around on top of the eyeballs. It's so cute! I can already envision a millipede as one of the new characters in my animation universe. I know once Samantha sees one in person, she's going to change her mind about them. But girls like Madison and her friends would whine and squeal and act like babies if I held a millipede in front of them.

"I love them! I want them all!" I look at Dad with the kind of face that sometimes gets him to buy things for me. It's an incredibly adorable face. But he just says to Lyle, "Do I need to buy a whole aquarium for one millipede?"

"Can I pick one up?" I ask Lyle before he can answer Dad's question. Lyle says I can, so while they talk, I put my hand into the case and hold it there, waiting for a millipede to crawl to me. One does, and I can feel every one of its thirty-six to four hundred legs tickling me as it climbs up my thumb and across my hand.

I look up to tell Dad how cool this is, then notice Terri a few rows away. She's holding a multicolored patchwork cat and petting it as she talks to a girl employee.

Millie the millipede (I've already named her) feels as good as the cat does, I bet. Terri may say she doesn't like creepy-crawly things, but she probably hasn't seen one like this close up.

I think she should.

Dad's too far away to ask, but I doubt he and Lyle would mind if I took Millie on a short walk.

As I get closer to Terri, I can hear her telling the Pets! Pets! Pets! girl that she's a cat person but her "boyfriend" has a dog. Hearing her use that word makes me want to barf a little.

I walk closer, gently closing my hand around Millie so she won't fall out. "Hi, Terri," I say.

"Oh, hi, Cleo," she says, like she didn't expect to see me. "Your dad told me you like cats. Isn't this one sweet?"

"I guess," I say. "But not as sweet as my millipede!" I open up my hand to show her. She sees it on my palm and screams like she's in a horror movie! At the same time, she tosses the cat into the air and it yowls and screeches. I rush to put my hand over Millie so she doesn't get hit by the falling cat. Terri and the girl put their hands out and the cat lands back in Terri's arms. Terri hugs it to her chest, whispering, "Oh my God, I'm so sorry." I don't know if she's talking to the cat, the girl, or my millipede.

"She would've landed on her feet anyway," the girl says. "This one's got good reflexes." She takes the cat from Terri and walks away, probably to where there's less excitement. Terri and I don't say or do anything. We just stand there looking at each other. I can see she's breathing heavily.

Suddenly Dad is standing with us. "What happened?" he asks.

"I showed Terri my millipede."

"Nothing happened," Terri tells Dad. "I was just surprised. I didn't mean to make a scene."

"I know *you* didn't," Dad says, glancing at me. He gives Terri a squeeze on the shoulder. "Let me take care of the millipede business and we'll go home."

"She's not coming to our house, is she?" I ask.

Dad frowns at me. "No, not tonight. But change that attitude, Cleo."

Ugh. Two *"change that attitude"*'s in one day. Now I'm going to have to be good for the rest of the night. Dad starts walking away, saying, "Come on," so I follow him back to the corner of the store.

Luckily he still buys me a millipede. Actually two! I'm thinking it's so Millie can have a friend, but Dad tells Lyle it's "for backup." I'm sitting behind Dad again as we drive back, but I don't care because I'm holding my millipedes in their new home—a small plastic terrarium with special soil and pieces of bark for them to hide under. Dad says he's sorry to Terri a few times, but I don't know why. Terri's the one who screamed and threw a cat in the air. And she said she *loved* cats. I wonder if we can believe anything she says.

We drive to Terri's house. She turns around to me before she leaves. "Have fun with your millipedes, Cleo," she says.

"They're not for fun," I tell her. "They're for research."

She laughs and gets out of the car. Dad walks up to her front door with her as I get out to sit in front. Before I get back in the car, I see them hugging. Yucch. And after they stop hugging, they kiss. Not a big, long, sloppy gross one, but definitely more than a good-night kiss. Why would any father find it appropriate for his eleven-year-old to see this?

Dad waits for her to walk inside, then comes back to the car and sees me frowning. "Cleo, I'm sorry . . . ," he says.

Yes! An apology!

"I'm sorry I brought Terri along like that tonight without preparing you. But she's going to be around a lot, and I'm going to make sure I have time for each of you. Individually and together. Okay?"

I nod, but I don't like the sound of this. Terri is not one of us, and I just don't think she'd add that much to our lives. Why can't Dad see that?

"So next time we see her, I expect you to be a lot nicer, kiddo."

"Okay," I say, but in my mind I'm not promising anything.

6

I wake up on Monday morning feeling different. At the beginning of every week since I started at Friendship Community School, there's always been an icky feeling in my belly. It knows something is going to go badly—that I'm going to do something dumb, or someone like Madison is going to make fun of me.

But today my stomach feels okay, all because of the hex Samantha and I did. I'm not truly expecting anything to happen, but it's still new and exciting and something to look forward to. Before I leave for school, I pat the voodoo doll on his head and straighten his tutu. And when I'm in the car—in the front where I belong—I can't help bouncing around in a way that I never would if someone like Madison was watching.

"You're in a strangely good mood," Dad says. "Why's that?"

I can't tell him the truth: *Well, Samantha and I decided to use the voodoo doll Uncle Arnie sent me—the voodoo doll you told me not to play with—to put a positive voodoo charm on her, and I can't wait to see if it works.* So I quickly come up with something that's true but not *quite* as truthful: "I'm glad I got two millipedes. And I had fun with Samantha when she came over."

I look at Dad to see if that story is good enough . . . and I can tell it is by the reaction on his face. "Her mom called afterward and said Sam had a great time too. She invited you to her house this coming weekend."

"Woo-hoo!" I shout, bouncing, until Dad tells me to calm down. When he drops me off and I run into the courtyard at school, I'm thinking this is going to be a pretty good day.

And it's okay, I guess—but nothing special happens to Samantha in our first class, history. I'm hoping something might go down at morning break, but it's nobody's birthday, so we don't get any sort of treat there. Instead we just sit at our desks like usual, eating our nutritious snacks and enriching our lives in our own personal way.

I'm quietly munching my pita chips when I hear a whisper from Madison. "Mmmm, yum yum yum," she says, making fake chewing sounds. "Cleo, don't you want any carrots?"

Sure enough, when I look over at Scabby Larry, he's chowing on his favorite little vegetable. Can't he eat anything else?

All animated villains have evil henchmen, and Madison

has her henchwomen, who join in the "fun." Lisa Lee makes chewing noises, throwing in a few "Ohio piggy" comments and snorts. Her face is tight and pointy, probably because her skin is being pulled back by the brown braid she always has at the back of her head. If I made her into a cartoon character, she'd be a rat. She always does the same things Madison does, a second later. Kylie Mae doesn't do anything specific. She doesn't ever really do anything, but she always has a sour frown on her face and these super-light blue eyes that make it look like she's thinking about absolutely nothing. I can't even imagine an animated animal for her. She'd be . . . a balloon.

I look toward the front of the classroom to see if Kevin's heard any of the comments or chewing sounds, but he has earbuds in. He must be enriching his life by listening to music during snack break.

I turn to Madison and her friends and stick my tongue out. My mouth is full of chewed-up chips and they squeal and "ewww" like the girly girls they are. Across the room, Samantha gives me a thumbs-up. It's an enjoyable moment, but more for me than Samantha, so we can't give the credit to voodoo.

Math class goes by without anything special either. Then Sam and I are walking across the lawn together like we always do, heading toward the lunchroom, when suddenly Sam stops. I keep walking but she grabs my arm.

"It's happening!" she says in an excited whisper.

"What is?" I ask.

"Take a sniff."

I sniff a few times, like a bunny rabbit with a dandelion, but I don't smell anything out of the ordinary.

"No, take a big breath in. Really sniff," Sam says.

I do. Then I smell what she smells.

She's right. It's happening.

Pizza!

My heart starts pounding and I can't hold back my smile from becoming big and goofy. "Oh my gosh!" I scream, jumping up and down.

"Pizza!" Sam shouts.

"Pizza!" I shout back, and we run toward the lunchroom. "A treat you can see and smell and taste *and* touch!"

The thing is, Monday is not pizza day. Monday is veggie stir-fry day, which is why I bring a sandwich because I only eat vegetables at dinnertime when Dad makes me. Pizza day only comes every couple of weeks, and never on a Monday. And Samantha loves the school pizza because it's the square kind with pepperonis that curl up around the edges and make little pools of grease.

I prefer triangular pizza to square pizza, so this treat is not as special for me. But it definitely is for Samantha, which means our hex worked! I can't believe we have to sit through the rest of the school day knowing what we know!

"This is unbelievable," Sam says at our lunch table, chewing happily on her greasy pizza.

"It tastes good?" I ask.

"Of course it tastes good," she says, "but that's not what I'm talking about."

"The hex! I know; I can't believe it!" It might be the most unbelievable thing that's happened to me in my whole entire life. My dad is wrong *and* voodoo is real!

"So what do we do next?" Sam asks, using her napkin to sop up one of the pepperoni's pools of grease. She says the grease is good for flavor but that eating it is unhealthy, which makes sense to me.

"What do you mean?" I ask.

"Well, it worked!" She looks around the lunchroom to make sure no one is listening, but of course no one is. Scabby Larry and a younger kid look like they're playing a game on a phone, and Madison and her friends are giggling, probably about something dumb. "So of course we have to do another hex," she says.

Another hex?

I never considered doing another, I guess because I didn't exactly plan on this one working. But Dad said not to mess with voodoo and I don't want him to be mad at me, so I'm not sure what to say.

Sam doesn't wait for me to answer. "I was thinking about this last night. . . ."

"Thinking about what?"

"I'm about to tell you," Sam says in between chews. "I

couldn't get to sleep and I was lying in bed wondering: what if the voodoo works? What will we do next?"

Of course she's already planning. Sam and her focus. She takes a breath like she's going to say something, but then she sighs, keeping me waiting. "Well?" I ask, impatient. "What?"

"I think we should . . ." She pauses. "Make ourselves popular."

Obviously the pizza grease has gone to Sam's head. Her brain is not working properly. "That's impossible," I say. "There's no way that little voodoo doll could do something like that." We look at each other for a second, neither of us saying anything.

Sam raises her eyebrows and takes another bite of pizza. "But maybe"—she finally says, pausing dramatically—"just maybe, it could."

I smile. If it *could,* it'd be great. Really, really great. Sam and I would have more friends than just each other. There'd be other people at our lunch table to share food and joke around and discuss triangular versus square pizza. And maybe I could wake up every morning like I did today. I'm sure Dad would like me to be happier at school. Then I could focus better, and get better grades, and be a better daughter—everything would be better, better, better!

"Okay," I say, feeling a tingle of anticipation. "If you think it *could* actually happen, how would we do it?"

"Well, who's the most popular girl in our grade?"

She knows the answer to that. "Maddy Paddy, duh," I say, rolling my eyes.

"Right. And if she did something—I don't know—something weird or embarrassing, people might not like her so much."

I lean in and concentrate, even putting down my turkey, lettuce, and butter sandwich so I can give Sam my full attention.

"If people made fun of *her* for doing something embarrassing," Sam whispers, "that might take some of the attention off us. It'd be good for you, it'd be good for me, it'd be good for everybody in Focus! It would really be good for the whole school if you think about it. And isn't that what the voodoo doll is for? Good?"

I'm impressed, and I tell her so. Samantha leans back in her chair, lifts her second piece of square pizza to her mouth, and takes a big chomp out of it. I've never seen her so happy.

Of course I hadn't thought of it her way. All I know is that Dad said to stay away from the voodoo, and it might've put a big scar on Uncle Arnie's hand. But Uncle Arnie didn't send me a spooky, scary doll; he sent me Positive Happy Voodoo Doll. That doll, with his stitched yarn mouth and silly pink tutu, brought Samantha her favorite pizza today.

And if he could make Madison do something so embarrassing in class it would make us popular, it could change my life—and Sam's—big-time. Nothing wrong with that! There's really no other choice but to try it.

"Okay," I say. "Let's do it."

Samantha's eyes look excited under her dark frizzy bangs. "Okay. So. How can you get Madison's hair?"

"Why *her* hair?" I ask. "It worked with your hair last time."

"Yeah, but I'd say this time we're hexing *her* to reach *our* goal. And you know what? This is going to be good for her too. She does something super embarrassing; she'll see what it's like to be you or me. She'll probably learn something from it."

"Okay," I agree. "But why am *I* getting her hair?" We've been talking about some wild things today, but that sounds ridiculously nuts. "I don't even like to go near her! Her teeth are so white and sparkly, I'm afraid they'll turn me blind!"

"Well, I haven't gone near her in years, so she'd find it pretty weird if I suddenly became her buddy and got real close and plucked a piece of hair out of her head. At least you're new."

I'm not sure I understand Samantha's logic. "So because I'm new, she won't think it's weird when *I* walk up to her and pull some hair out of her head?"

Sam's speedy brain has this all figured out already, of course. "You sit behind Madison in science lab tomorrow, right?"

I do sit behind Madison, and sometimes I can't pay

attention to Kevin's experiments because her perfect golden hair hypnotizes me. I imagine how often she must wash it, and how expensive her shampoo must be, and how she probably has a maid or butler to comb it a thousand times for her every night.

"So just sneeze or something, and grab a piece of her hair," Sam says, again like it's the easiest thing in the world.

I'm not totally sure this will work, but when I see the look on Samantha's face and I think about our future, full of all the positive happy juju, mojo, gris-gris, or hoodoo that popularity will bring, I know I will give it my best try.

7

Samantha must still have the taste of pizza on her lips because she's smiling for the next couple of hours. Neither of us, however, is thrilled when it's time for Recreational Wellness. It's what normal schools would call Phys Ed and we strongly *don't like* gym. I don't want to lose my breath and play stupid games in front of the whole class. Even worse, I have to get changed in a locker room in front of all the girls.

But Samantha always figures out a way to make it fun. Today she walks over to my locker like she's a model and says, "Fresh from Paris, it's the stunning Mirabelle Escoofay, wearing the latest in Phys Ed fashion!"

Normally I wouldn't goof around like this, but Sam's so confident, it rubs off on me. So I jump up and suck my cheeks in all skinny and start walking like a model too, with a snotty smirk on my face.

"Where would these two be modeling? *Mars?*" asks Madison from across the locker room, and her sidekick friends laugh like always.

I feel like a balloon that's just been untied—all my model air comes hissing out. Not Samantha. She starts talking in a robot voice and says, "Yes, I am the most beautiful Martian model in the universe, and I have come to kill mean Earthlings." I laugh, but I'm too embarrassed to add any more. Then our Recreational Wellness teacher, Janet, blows a whistle and says it's time to go out to the gym. As Madison walks off, I hear her mutter, "So stupid." But when Samantha looks at me with her arms still held up stiff like a robot, I don't care about Madison at all. I just think about how she's going to have one less hair tomorrow after science lab! And after we do the charm, one less hair for Madison will equal lots more happiness for us!

Samantha and I practically skip into the gym, but once again my happiness hisses away. Sitting on the floor in between the two basketball nets is a gigantic white ball, big as a tire on an eighteen-wheeler. I know what's coming next.

"Crab soccer, everyone!" shouts Janet.

Samantha and I frown at each other. Crab soccer is, in a word, horrible. Everyone gets down on all fours, but not facedown like a dog. We're faceup, like a crab. Then you have to crawl around, kicking the gigantic ball with your crab legs until it goes into the other team's goal. How is this supposed to make us better human beings? How is this supposed to teach us about sportsmanship and teamwork? All I know is that it makes the inside of your elbows hurt and gets your shorts all dirty because, let's face it, even though you're not supposed to drag your butt on the floor of the gym, it's hard not to.

Janet divides us into teams, and Samantha's on the opposite one, along with Madison. "Goodbye, Martian model," Samantha says in her robot voice, then crawls to the other side of the gym. I see Madison roll her eyes.

Janet blows the whistle and tosses the big ball into the center of the gym. All of us crabs start crawling around, and I wonder: *If a Martian model really did come down and watch this, what would she think? Would she try to learn from us, or would she blow us all away and then report to the king of Mars how stupid we all look down here?*

"What are you *doing?*" Madison yells, suddenly reminding me that I'm in the middle of a crab soccer game. She's trying to get around me to the ball, but I'm just sitting there. "Pick up your bony butt and get out of my way!"

Right then I decide that there's nothing more I want to do in the world than kick that huge ball into Madison's goal and force my team to cheer for me. She and I get to the ball at the same time and kick it until it winds up in the corner of the gym. We're both kicking and kicking, but the ball isn't going anywhere.

Suddenly I hear a scream. "Waaaah! Cleo kicked me!" Madison is curled up on the ground holding her leg. "She couldn't get the ball out of the corner, so she kicked me!"

I didn't kick her, not even close, and her whining is so fake I can almost see her snickering at me. It makes me wish I had a pin to prick her with like the voodoo doll!

And in that exact moment, as Janet is blowing her whistle and the rest of our crab teammates are confused, I know I can do it. While Madison's rolling on the ground, fake crying, tossing around her perfect flowing hair, I reach out my fingers and pluck a piece right out of her head. My aim isn't perfect, though, so I might actually get two or three. Ha ha, Maddy Paddy!

"Now she pulled my hair! Cleo kicked me, and then she pulled my hair!"

"That's so not true!" I yell, even though half of it *is* true.

"Cleo," says Janet. She's got a real serious sound in her voice, like Dad when I forget to feed Toby or I break a dish. "Go to the locker room *right now.* I'll deal with you after I send Madison to the nurse." Then Janet's voice gets all friendly when she turns to Madison. "That is, if you can walk. Can you walk, Madison?"

"I'll . . . try," Madison says, sniffling.

I can't believe her! She's such a Fakey Fakerson! So I yell something. It's not on purpose; I just *do* it. It begins with *holy* and ends with something like *poop.* But it's not *poop;* it's a bad word. I didn't mean to say it; I just can't believe what's happening.

"Cleo!" shouts Janet, harsher than before. "Go to the locker room!"

As I stomp off, I see Janet holding her hand out to Madison, and Madison pretending like it's hard to get up. I'm mad at first, but once I'm alone between the lockers, my mood gets better—because when I open my left hand, I see *three* pieces of Madison Paddington's hair!

I open my locker with my right hand and pull out my science notebook. Between my drawings and my pages of millipede notes is a plastic folder. Like a scientist working with dangerous materials, I carefully pick up each individual hair and slide them inside one by one. I'd like to stand there and admire them for a while, but I realize I'd better change and wait for Janet like I'm ashamed of what just happened.

Janet is more serious than angry. She tells me to go to the principal's office and sit on the chair outside. My dad will meet me there. He was going to have to pick me up soon anyway, but I've never gotten in this much trouble before and I hope he's not too mad.

Luckily the principal, Frederick, doesn't want to talk to me. I have to sit in a hallway in the courtyard as all the other kids walk by on their way to their parents' or nannies' cars. I can tell that some of them are talking about me by the way they look over, but I'm not embarrassed. I'm kind of proud. I may be in trouble, but that's a small price to pay for what the final result is going to be. A whole new life of fun and friends and good times all the time!

Samantha walks by and gives me a concerned look. I start to give her a thumbs-up but change my mind when I see Dad walking toward me. His mouth is a straight line above his chin.

"You know I don't want to talk to the principal, right?" he asks.

"Yes," I say, acting sorry.

While Dad's gone, I read from a library book I got on millipedes. I learn that when millipedes are threatened, they coil up into a tight ball. The picture in the book reminds me of Madison curled up on the gym floor pretending to be hurt. But of course the millipede is *much* more attractive than Madison.

Dad's only in Frederick's office for a few minutes; then he walks out toward the parking lot. "Come on, let's go home," he says, already way ahead of me. We get in the car without talking at all. I figure it's best if I wait for Dad to start.

He doesn't say anything as he drives us home. He just listens to a talky podcast while I stare out the window. When the story ends much later, he looks over at me.

"Listen, I know you've been having a hard time since we moved here," he says. "It's not easy to move across the country to a new place. Go to a new school, make new friends.

And meeting Terri was a big deal that you probably weren't ready for. So I can understand why you might act out and get in some trouble."

Wow. I thought Dad was going to be mad, but it sounds like he's blaming himself. This is the best!

"But I don't want any more of it, Cleo. No more bad behavior." Sounding more serious now, he continues, "It is *not* okay to say those kinds of words. In school or anywhere."

"I know. I won't do it again."

"Don't make promises you can't keep," Dad says.

"Okay. I promise I'll *try* not to do it again."

"Good," says Dad. Then it's quiet for a minute. I think that's all he's going to say!

I can see he's not too upset, so I wonder if he can take a joke. "Can I say 'poo'?" I ask, all sweet and innocent.

Dad laughs out loud. "Yes, you can say 'poo.'"

"I won't say 'poo,'" I tell him. "That's for losers."

"Don't say 'loser.' That's not right," says Dad, but he's still kind of joking. So I ask him what words I can say. He says no to *fart hole,* but yes to *butt noodle.* Yes to *booger snot,* but no to *crap ferret.* We start laughing and Dad turns on music, which is better than a podcast any day.

Back home he tells me to start on my homework, but it's hard because when I open my science notebook, all I want to do is stare at those three long blond hairs. And my voodoo doll is standing nearby on top of my dresser, waiting to be put to good use. But it's one of Dad's rules that I can only get together with Samantha on weekends, so I'm going to have to wait four more days before we can cast our spell using "the power of two." Four loooooong days that are going to feel like forever.

After today, though, I can't ask Dad for any favors. So I do my whining on the inside.

Samantha and I spend the rest of the week sneaking in conversations about the you-know-what we're going to put on you-know-who. You-know-who stays away from me, probably because she knows I could always grab her hair again! Sometimes, across the classroom or playground, I see her and her friends looking in my direction with their faces scrunched up like unfriendly weasels, but that's way better than picking on me.

Dad grounds me, sort of, for saying the bad word in Recreational Wellness. He actually makes me *do* all my chores (instead of doing them halfway), and I can't use our tablet for drawing or playing games. But it's not so bad; I spend the extra time with my millipedes. I add twigs and grass from the backyard to their terrarium to make it a real home. I learn online that there are both boy and girl millipedes and, using a magnifying glass to look at their private parts, I discover that Millie is a boy. The one I named Marty is a girl. I think so anyway. It's hard to tell because everything's so small.

I also watch them crawl around in their box and chew on little pieces of apple and banana. Because millipedes have weak mouth parts, Dad and I had to slice and peel the food, then leave it out for a couple of days. They like rotten fruit best, which is funny because I don't even like fresh fruit.

In bed on Friday night, I can't stop thinking about how tomorrow is Saturday. This charm is going to be so much bigger and more important than Sam's pizza. That only brought her happiness for thirty-five minutes, the length of lunchtime. The next one could bring us happiness for more minutes than we'll ever be able to count! I've heard people say that they feel like they have butterflies in their stomach when they're excited, but I don't have tiny, feathery butter-flies. I have hummingbirds buzzing all over. Or ostriches running around.

The hummingbirds and ostriches are keeping me awake, though, pecking at my brain with questions. What if it wasn't real? What if the pizza was a coincidence? What if I'm getting my hopes up for nothing?

I want to talk to someone about all this stuff, but I can't call Sam. It's late and her mom might hear her phone ring. There's only one other person in the world who knows what I'm going through, and once I get *that* thought in my head,

I can't shake it. I won't be able to sleep until I actually talk to him.

I sneak through the house to the dining room, where Dad's desk is. I turn on his main computer and it makes a loud musical sound. I jump back, then scramble to turn down the volume.

I see the link Dad uses to call Uncle Arnie, and I click on it. It rings five, six, seven times, seeming louder with every ring. Finally, the screen on the other end of the line pops up. It's just black, though, until one little light turns on and a stream of light hits a table or a desk. Whatever it is, it's crammed with papers and files and wind-up toys and who knows what else. Exactly like my dad's desk.

"Helloooooo?" a voice asks. It's a guy off camera, sounding kind of like an owl.

"Hi," I whisper. "Is that Uncle Arnie?"

His face suddenly fills the screen. He's got fuzzy black-and-gray hair shooting off his head from every angle, making my messy head look as beautiful as Madison's. Similar-looking hair shoots off his chin in tufts. It's not enough to be called a beard, though; it's just fuzz.

"Is that my little niece? Cleooooooo! I don't think I've ever gotten a call from you before. Look how grown up you are! What's up, mah girl?"

"Shhh! My dad's asleep," I warn him.

"Okay, I'll keep it down," he says, quieter. "But do you mind if I turn on another light?"

I doubt that would be a problem, so I say okay. That's when I see the rest of his room. It's a little like our house—but even messier. There's shelf after shelf crammed with books from the floor to the ceiling. But there are also picture frames and snow globes and voodoo dolls and other fun things, like a guitar and a banjo and a couple of keyboards on the floor, and a fat black-and-white cat strolling across the desk. Everything looks dusty, even the cat.

"I bet you have some questions about your birthday present," he says.

"Yeah," I say. Then all the words come flooding out of my mouth; I have no control over them. "My friend Sam and I did a charm and it worked—at least, I'm pretty sure it worked—but now we want to do another one and Dad says it's not real and not to get mixed up in it, but it wasn't bad, it was good! Really good! So it might be real. Is it, Uncle Arnie?"

He smiles big and I'm pretty sure I see some spinach or something between his teeth. "Of course it's real, honey! Positive Happy Voodoo Doll is the next big thing in voodoo. It does good instead of evil. You have to be focused, be strong, and *be*-lieve. Get it? Believe!"

I'm not totally understanding what he's saying, but he's got so much enthusiasm, I could listen to him forever. Then suddenly I'm remembering that I'm in our dining room in the middle of the night using a computer I'm not supposed to use. Now I'm more worried about getting caught than about asking a bunch of questions about voodoo.

My uncle doesn't know that, though, so he keeps blabbing. "You had moved to a new state—California of all places, with all those strange rangers—and I thought the doll would be a great way for you to bond with a friend and create some fun mojo. . . ."

"Okay, thanks, Uncle Arnie." All I really wanted to know was if our hex was real, and it was! "I guess I'd better go back to bed. . . ."

"Cleo, don't go yet!" he shouts, then quiets down again. "There's a rule I forgot to put in the instructions. You already know that Positive Happy Voodoo Doll is all about the power of two, the power of friendship, right?"

I nod and let him go on. "Here's the thing. Once two friends have lain . . . laid? Once two friends have lain—no, laid—their hands upon the doll's body with their hex, no others shall touch the doll until the spell has come to fruition. That one's a biggie."

I don't know what *fruition* means, but instead of asking, I think about the context of the sentence, like we once learned in English class. It must mean when the spell comes true.

"You're not saying much, little niece," Uncle Arnie says. "Do ya get it?"

I'm sure my face is saying, *Huh?* But I just nod and say, "Yeah."

"Don't forget that. No others!" He nods, like he's convinced himself he made his point. "Okay, I'll let you go, then. Tell that fancy-pants brother of mine to get in touch more often, okay? And tell him Fuzzer says hello!" Uncle Arnie scoops up his fat cat and holds him next to his face, making his paw wave goodbye. I say goodbye, and realize as I turn off the computer that Uncle Arnie and Fuzzer look exactly alike.

Inside Sam's condo building, Dad rings the doorbell and Samantha's mom answers it, dressed up again in a skirt and a tight blouse—on a Saturday! I don't know how she does it. At our house, Saturday is for sloppiness. Actually, every day is for sloppiness in our house. Fashion wasn't particularly my thing before now, but maybe I could learn something from spending time with Samantha's mom. It might be good for Dad too, since he only wears T-shirts and shorts. Paige is exactly the kind of person you want to know when you live in Los Angeles. If I looked as glamorous as she does, I bet I could be popular *without* voodoo.

"Nice to see you, Cleo. Bradley. Come on in." She asks if Dad wants to stay for a while, but he says he can't; he has work to do.

"Come a little early to pick her up, then. Have a drink or something."

"Thanks, Paige, I'll see if I can," says Dad. I notice her perfect fingernails again as she squeezes his arm, and I wonder if Terri would like Dad having a drink with Paige. I wish he would!

After he leaves, Samantha's mom asks if we'd like some Cokes. I know *I* would, but Dad doesn't let me have high-fructose corn syrup; he says it's not healthy for you. But when I ask Samantha's mom if she has anything without high-fructose corn syrup, she laughs like it's the funniest thing she's ever heard. She doesn't think my dad would get mad if I had only one. I don't know if she's right, but I decide to believe her because, well, I want a Coke!

Sam and I pop open our sodas and run to her room, which is perfect for voodoo hexing. Unlike the rest of their perfectly clean white condo, it's a dark purple cave with the windowsills and door painted black. Her comforter and pillows are black with bright pink splashes all over them. And her posters and decorations have a cool skeleton theme. She told me her dad sends her tons of little skeleton toys from Mexico, where he lives. I guess when you look around Samantha's room, it's not all that shocking that she was so interested in my voodoo doll.

"So. Did you bring it?" she asks.

I unzip my backpack and Samantha pulls out the doll. We both stare at it for a second. Dad thinks it's still a toy with yarn hair, button eyes, and a pin in its stomach. But we know what he really is. We know he's powerful.

"Did you bring Madison's you-know-whats?" Sam asks.

"Of course, duh!" I say, taking out the clear folder with the three hairs inside.

I carefully pull out one piece of hair. I hand it to Samantha, who wraps it around a piece of yarn on the doll's head. We're so careful; it's like we're surgeons on one of those hospital shows Dad and I sometimes watch. "So, should we do this one the same way as last time?" Sam asks.

"Yep," I say. "All we need to do is *be* focused and *be*-lieve, and something else that starts with *be*. I forget."

Sam has no idea what I'm talking about, and I don't bother to explain. Instead I pull the instructions out of my backpack and look at them carefully. "Number one. We've decided who deserves it."

"Right. Popularity is deserved by us!" says Sam.

"Number two, you put the hair on the doll. So for number three, we have to decide where we would like the desired result to occur, and put the pin there."

"Well, we want the popularity, but Madison needs to be embarrassed first. That could happen anywhere on her body. So I guess we can put it anywhere, right?" Sam asks.

"Sounds good to me," I say. "Where should we put it?"

"His butt!" Sam says happily.

"Why?"

"Well, the instructions say it doesn't matter, but maybe something embarrassing could happen to Madison, like she pulls a butt muscle or falls on her butt."

"And when we become popular, people will kiss *our* butts!" I laugh.

"Right!" Sam agrees. "So, are we ready?"

We put the doll on the floor between us. "Can I do the pin this time?" I ask Sam.

"Sure," she says, handing it to me. I hold it between my fingers and take a deep breath. The doll's butt is a few inches away from me, waiting for a pin. But I can't poke it, not yet, because I'm wondering if this is the right thing to do. Uncle Arnie said the doll is meant for good things, and this hex isn't good for Madison. It won't make Madison's life better. But then I remember her perfect hair and puffy lips and piggy snorts and clown comments, and I know what I need to do. Madison's life doesn't need to be better; *ours* does! And when I imagine me and Samantha being popular—no one calling us names or making fun of Focus!—I do it. I poke the pin in the doll's butt—and it feels good.

I look down and start concentrating. What will it be like to be popular? I never have been, not even in Ohio, so I don't know how it works. First I imagine people waving at us when we walk across the courtyard and wanting to sit with us at lunch. Kids would come to our houses on weekends and we'd have our own special inside jokes. And if Madison got embarrassed by something, especially something butt-related, everyone would stop thinking she was so great.

Before I know it, Sam decides that five minutes is up, and I'm sorry I don't get to dream more about popularity. We spend the next hour laughing and drinking Coke and talking about other things, like our science projects. Sam has decided to go with her idea about saving the environment. She says the glaciers are melting and if we don't stop them, polar bears and penguins won't have any place to live. That sounds so serious. It makes me glad I chose millipedes!

We also talk about Terri and how much I don't like my dad liking her. Sam understands because her mom and dad got divorced a long time ago. She spends most of the year with her mom but sometimes visits her dad for weekends or the summer in Mexico.

"What's that like?" I ask.

"Oh, it can be great," she tells me. "Like, I get two sets of presents for my birthday and Christmas. Or if one of them won't get me something, the other one might. But it can be hard too. I miss my dad when I'm here, and then I miss my mom when I'm with him."

I sort of understand what she means. I don't really *miss* my mom since I never knew her, but sometimes it's a little lonely with only Dad and Toby. But that doesn't mean I want someone like Terri coming in and changing things. It would be so much better if Dad liked Paige instead. I might learn how to brush my hair without hurting it, or to paint my nails cool colors and not bite them, or even to shop in Beverly Hills and try to look decent in designer clothes.

"Has your mom ever had a boyfriend like my dad has a girlfriend?" I ask.

"Oh yeah, she's had a lot," Sam says.

"Did she ever have a boyfriend you didn't like?"

"Oh, for sure! Some have been okay, but others have been icky. Or dumb. Or losers. Or too tall."

"What do you do when it's one of those?" I ask.

"I'm sour and rude to them, and after a while they go away."

"What if they don't?"

"Well, she doesn't have a boyfriend now, so it must work!" Samantha laughs, and I laugh along with her. Sour and rude; I can do that. I'll just think of Kylie Mae and her lemon-sucking face.

Sam and I are having such a good time that I don't even realize Dad has come to pick me up until I hear Samantha's mom's voice close by, saying "They're down here in Samantha's room. They've barely come up for air the whole time. They've probably been working on their science projects; they've been very intent on something. . . ."

Oh no! The voodoo doll is lying right on the carpet, where anybody could see. With the speed of a cheetah, I dive onto the ground and shove the doll under Sam's bed—at the exact moment Sam's mom opens the door with Dad by her side.

Dad looks around. "I think these two girls have been up to no good," he says.

Sitting on the floor next to each other, Samantha and I look up. How could Dad know?

"Why do you say that?" Samantha's mom asks.

"Coke cans!" Dad says, kidding around. "I normally don't let Cleo have soda."

"Yes, she was a very good girl and told me that, but I figured they could have a treat since it's a special night. Actually, I could pop one open for you while Cleo packs up her things and says goodbye."

"No thanks," says Dad, "but I wouldn't mind a glass of water. Get your things, Cleo. We'll head out in a minute." He and Sam's mom walk off down the hallway.

I carefully put the doll in my backpack as Samantha and I look at each other with relief.

We did it. Now we just have to wait.

9

It's hard to keep my mind on anything besides the hex, especially when I look at the voodoo doll's button eyes staring at me from my dresser. But Dad finds a way to distract me on Sunday.

"Terri's coming over tonight," he says, poking his head into my room, where I'm drawing a super-long millipede character to add to my animation empire. It's a lot of work because I'm trying to put different kinds of shoes on all his feet. I'm busy. I don't need interruptions.

"Look respectable," Dad says. "No bank robbery masks. And clean your room."

"Clean my room?"

"Yes. It'll do you good." Then he turns around and walks away.

"She's not coming in my room, is she?" I ask, following him down the hall.

Dad stops and sighs. "She may not come in your room, but this is her first visit to the house, and I might like to show her around." I can tell he's getting impatient because he's pulling pieces of his hair up and away from his head. I follow him toward his dining room office and I'm shocked by what I see.

Our living room and dining room are totally clean. Dad's computers aren't dusty and boxes of junk are pushed along the wall instead of in the middle of the room. His desk isn't covered with papers. There's no Toby fur on the floor.

He must really like Terri.

"Please, Cleo?" Dad asks. He looks so helpless and hopeful, I give in and force myself to go to my room. I move piles of things into corners, into my closet, and under my bed. I don't make the bed, but I flatten out the comforter. That's plenty.

Far down the hall, I hear our doorbell ring. It's her. Toby runs and barks like a wild wolf. I hope he jumps on her with his dirty paws, but I guess he doesn't because I hear her saying, "Hello, boy, you must be Toby! I've heard a lot about you! You're a pretty boy, aren't you?"

I'm sure Toby knows better than to believe her. Dad tells him to settle down; then he says hi to Terri and I hear a kissing noise. Gross.

"Cleo! Terri's here!" Dad shouts, like I'm supposed to be happy about it.

"I'm busy!" I yell back.

"Come out here!" Dad shouts again. "She brought something for us!"

I don't really care what Terri brought, but since it could be cookies or money or a monkey T-shirt, I go. I walk down the hallway slowly to make them wait, but they're not waiting at all. They're in the kitchen, where Dad is putting a bottle of wine on the counter while Terri takes a sip from her glass.

I think of something rude to say, like Sam suggested. "That looks like you're drinking pee."

"Cleo!" Dad says in a scolding voice, but I go on.

"Don't get too close to the stove, Terri," I say, though it's not even on. "We wouldn't want you to burn your hand like my uncle Arnie did."

She gives Dad a confused look, and he explains. "Uncle Arnie said years ago that his hand had gotten burned because of a voodoo curse." Dad turns to me. "But we know that's not true now, right, Cleo?"

"Yeah, yeah," I say quickly, sorry I brought it up. With our latest hex out there waiting to make us popular, I do *not* want to be talking voodoo with them.

"This crazy brother of mine who lives in New Orleans, he's into spirits and voodoo and all that stuff. He even sent Cleo a voodoo doll for her birthday! Of course she knows it's not real. Right, Cleo?"

I nod. I've got to change the subject! So I turn to Terri and ask, "So, what did you bring me?"

Dad says, "Rude." And I wasn't even trying that time!

Terri doesn't seem to care, though. "I actually brought it for all of us," she says, walking toward our kitchen table. "It's a game we could play."

I usually like the games we play in Focus!, but I just sit back and wait for her to impress me. She shows me the box. It's a game called Pig Mania.

In my mind I see Madison making a pig face with her pinkie finger and her friends oinking and snorting.

"I don't like pigs," I say. "Pigs are dirty and smelly and from Ohio, and that's not cool."

"Cleo," Dad says. "Remember what you and I talked about?"

Dad and I talk about a lot of things all the time, but I guess he means I'm supposed to be nice to her. Ugh.

"Actually, pigs are very clean animals," Terri says, "and these ones are little and plastic and pretty cute." She pulls out a cup that says "Pig Sty" on it, and rolls out two tiny pigs.

They *are* pretty cute, but I'm going to keep that to myself.

Terri explains that the object of the game is to roll the pigs to score the most points. I don't understand and I say so, but Dad tells me to keep listening. She shows us how the little pigs can land in different positions, and the weirder the position, the more points you get. So if one lands on its nose, it's called a Snouter and you get ten points. On its feet it's a Hoofer—five points. On its nose and ear it's a Leaning Jowler, and that's fifteen points. The hard part of the game is deciding to stop rolling, because if one pig lands on its left side and the other one lands on its right, you "Pig Out" and lose all your points from that roll.

"Sounds kind of dumb," I say, though I actually think it could be fun.

"What could possibly be dumb about rolling pigs and scoring points? It's the most brilliant idea in the world!" Dad jokes, shaking the cup with the pigs. "Come on, Cleo, we don't want to play alone!"

"Okay, I guess. One game."

Terri rolls first and she only scores ten points before she pigs out. She groans and hands the cup to Dad. He rolls twenty, decides to keep the points, and passes the pigs to me. Unlike Terri and Dad, I am an awesome roller. I rack up forty points without pigging out, and Terri says she's never seen anything like it. I get up to sixty-five points and I only need one hundred total to win. Dad tells me to think about stopping, but I can't.

A few rolls later, it happens. I pig out! All my hard work is now worth nothing. I scream. Terri screams . . . and then says the bad word I said in Recreational Wellness! I look at her in shock.

"Dad, did you hear that?"

"I couldn't help it," she says, laughing. "Sorry."

Even though I just lost a lot of points, I'm kind of

laughing too because Terri takes this pig game seriously enough to say a bad word.

We keep playing. Dad makes me add up everyone's points, which is annoying but not as terrible as doing math problems because at least there's possible winning involved.

I learn to not be so greedy and try to stop rolling when I get to twenty points or so. With a couple more rolls, I win the game. As I'm cheering and dancing around the kitchen, Terri says that it's beginner's luck.

"No, it's not," I tell her. "I won fair and square."

"She's kidding, Cleo," Dad says. Then he tells me it's time for bed. I groan, but I start to go. Slowly. I mean, Terri's not great, but neither is bedtime.

"Hey," Dad says. "Why don't you show Terri your room before you hit the sack?"

"Do I have to?" I ask. One fun game with pigs is not going to change the way I feel about Dad's *girlfriend.*

"Yes, you have to." Dad turns to Terri and adds, "Cleo's got some really good artwork you might like."

Since I have no choice, I let Terri follow me to my room. She notices Marty and Millie in their terrarium but turns her eyes away to the drawings and paintings and things pinned on my bulletin board.

"Who's this?" Terri asks, pointing at the picture of my mom in her blue floppy hat.

What is she doing looking at my mom? "That's my

mom, and she's the only mom I'll ever have," I snap at her. "That picture's going to be up there forever."

"It should be," Terri says. "She's pretty. You two have the same smile."

Terri's right about that of course.

"What's this?" she asks, pointing at one of my new Pandaroo masterpieces.

I like talking about my drawings, but this time I do it in my unfriendliest voice. "He's one of the characters I created for my animation career. He travels through the galaxy and shoots rainbows out of his butt."

"It almost looks like the rainbow is the energy that's propelling him through space," she says. That's kind of a cool idea, but I keep that thought to myself.

"I'm working on some animation with him on the computer," I say.

"Oh, can I see?" she asks, acting all interested when I'm sure she'd much rather be with Dad drinking wine and making smoochy noises.

"I don't know," I say. "I only just started so I'm not very good at it yet."

"Hey, if it's anything like your drawings, it'll be great!"

"O . . . kay." I drag myself to my desk, sit down with a thump, and click around on my computer. "But all he's doing is moving across the screen and he's real jumpy. . . ."

When I turn around, Terri is looking at the other things

in my room. She picks up one of my robots and rolls her hands across the wheels under its feet. She squeezes a monster doll and it makes a growling noise. "That's spooky-looking. What is that?" she asks.

She's walking toward my dresser!

"Is that the doll your uncle sent you?"

She's heading for the voodoo doll!

In my head, I immediately hear the voice of Uncle Arnie: *"No others shall touch the doll until the spell has come to fruition . . . no others . . . no others . . ."*

"No others" means Terri!

Her hand is reaching out to touch the doll, just like she touched all the other things in my room without asking.

"Don't touch it!" I yell. I jump out of my chair and grab the doll from the top of my dresser before she can get to it. "This is a very special and precious gift from my uncle, and it's not meant for anyone's hands except mine and Sam's!"

Terri seems surprised. "Sorry, I didn't know. It looked cool."

"It *is* cool," I snap. "I told Dad you shouldn't come in my room and I was right!"

"Okay," she says, heading toward the hallway. "Well, thanks for playing Pig Mania with us."

"Yeah, whatever."

"Good night." Terri closes the door behind her.

I can feel my heart punching the inside of my chest as I put the doll in its box and slide it under my bed where random people can't see and touch it. I change into my pajamas and lie down on my bed without getting under the covers. I stare at the ceiling because I'm not tired enough to close my eyes. Dad and Terri are talking in the kitchen, but I can't make out any real words. Then I hear footsteps coming toward my door.

"Cleo, are you all right?" Dad asks. "Do you want me to tuck you in?"

"No. You go talk with *Terri*."

"Do you want me to come in so we can talk?"

"No," I say, though I have plenty I'd like to tell him— like that Terri should go home, and soon. I'd like to say that I didn't want to clean my room for her, I didn't want to play a game with her, and she could have ruined the very important hex Samantha and I put so much work into. But I definitely can't tell him that one.

"You're sure you don't want a good-night kiss?" Dad asks from the other side of the door.

"No," I say. "I'll see you in the morning."

"Okay. Love you."

I don't feel like saying "I love you" back tonight. So I just say, "Good night."

10

I fall asleep mad, but I wake up early—earlier than my alarm even—feeling just fine. Who cares about Terri when today Sam and I might become popular?

Unlike a normal morning, when Dad has to yell at me two or three times before I'll pull my comforter off my head, today I jump out of bed and get dressed, say "good morning" to Marty and Millie, and then go make toast for my morning peanut butter and jelly sandwich. When I throw my knife into the sink and it makes a loud clang, Dad yells from his bedroom, "Cleo, what are you doing?"

"Making breakfast!" I shout back. "Want some?"

I don't hear his answer, but a few minutes later he slowly walks into the kitchen in his underwear and a T-shirt, with his hair messed up and thick glasses on. "Don't make us late, Dad," I warn him.

"You're in a good mood, considering how you were acting last night," he says.

"Oh yeah." I'm not sure *what* to tell him about last night.

"That's all you can say? Oh yeah?"

"She was touching all the stuff in my room," I try to explain. "Like my monsters and my robots, and she didn't ask." I don't mention the voodoo doll.

"Well, there are better ways to deal with something like that," Dad says. "You need to apologize the next time you see her."

I don't know about that, Dad, I'm thinking, but I just nod.

"She really liked playing the game with you," he tells me—which means Terri is kind of dumb because I wasn't that nice to her then either. "I'd like you to give her a chance."

"Okay!" I say, impatient. I don't want to talk; I want to go to school! "Are you ready to go?"

"Give me a couple of minutes, for Pete's sake," he says. "What's the occasion?"

I'm sure Dad has no idea about the hex, but I'd better stop being so excited or he's going to realize something is strange. "Nothing," I say. "I've got a lot to discuss with Samantha. You know, our science projects and stuff."

"Well, let me make my coffee and we'll get going."

"Okay, but hurry!" I shove the last piece of PB&J into my mouth and run down the hall to get my backpack and jacket. I go and sit in our car and open my notebook to the stuff I should have read for Focus! class over the weekend.

Dad finally comes out of the house and drives me to school. When I get to our classroom, I look at Samantha and I know we're thinking the same things: *What's going to happen to make us popular? What is Madison going to do to embarrass herself? How will it happen? When?*

It's super hard to concentrate in any of our classes because I can't stop looking over at Madison. One time she catches me. She doesn't stick her tongue out because she's eating her lightly salted kale chips like a perfect princess, but she shoots me a look that everybody knows—the look that says "What do you want, weirdo?" I turn my eyes away, and a second later I hear a cough!

Sam and I look at each other. Maybe a lightly salted kale chip is getting caught in Madison's throat and she has to cough it out! Even better, maybe Kevin will have to do the Heimlich and grab her around the stomach and squeeze hard to force it out of her! We tried to learn the Heimlich maneuver at my old school. It was totally embarrassing to practice on each other, and it would be way worse if someone had to use it on you in class for real. Everyone would see the piece of food come flying out of your mouth, and what if it landed on someone and . . . ?

But Madison's not coughing anymore.

At lunch, Sam and I watch carefully as Madison exits

the cafeteria line and walks toward her table. She stumbles a tiny bit.

"Did she trip? Was that a little trip?" I wonder out loud to Sam.

"If you have to ask, it's definitely not embarrassing enough to count." Sam is frowning. She's disappointed and so am I. If nothing happens to Madison today, we may have to decide that pizza day was a coincidence. But Uncle Arnie said it was real, and I want to believe him. Our popularity hangs in the balance!

Late in the day, Kevin says it's time for the Focus! kids to head to our classroom. Scabby Larry jumps out of his chair, like there are hundred-dollar bills waiting for us there. Sam and I, we take our time. We're in no rush.

I expect Madison to make a comment about me and Scabby Larry going to Focus! together, but she's actually standing up too. I guess she needs to go to the bathroom. It would be great if she got stuck in the toilet and they had to call the janitor, and the whole school gathered around and it ended up on the TV news. Now *that* would be embarrassing!

When we get to Focus!, there's the usual noise and activity because kids from all different grades are arriving and settling in. Roberta tells us to take our seats and quiet down because we have a special presentation today.

"I know it's difficult to believe that you can achieve your dreams when you're a kid here in middle school," says

Roberta. "But this is where it begins. If you start accomplishing goals now, you'll get used to doing it. Then you'll do it your entire life and be as successful as you want to be! So I would like to introduce you to a middle school student who is exceptionally focused on realizing her dreams. Most of you probably know her. Please welcome Madison Paddington."

The classroom door opens and Madison struts in like a celebrity on the red carpet. Everyone in class looks at each other like the Martian king has landed or Pandaroo has jetted in on his trail of rainbows. Why in the world would Madison be here? Maybe she hit Roberta's car with her bike or killed Roberta's cat or something and owes her a favor. Otherwise Maddy Paddy would never set foot in the Focus! room.

Madison stands up straight and proud next to Roberta's desk as Roberta says, "Madison is here today to share some of the great ways she manages to achieve her goals."

Samantha leans over to me and whispers, "My goal is to be mean and nasty to people, and I achieve it every day!" I laugh so loud I can't help snorting. Everyone looks at me, including Madison.

Roberta makes a squinty-eyed face at me as she says to everyone, "Please, let's give our fellow student all our attention."

Though none of us want to, we all quiet down. Madison doesn't look nervous at all to speak in front of the class.

"When Roberta was looking for a student to talk to the Focus! class, of course everybody thought of me. I have been an achiever from a very young age. One of my goals is to be the captain of the high school cheerleading squad, so in second grade, I started cheering for the local peewee football team. Unfortunately I fell from the top of a human pyramid. I told the coach that the girls on the bottom row were too small to hold the rest of us, but the coach didn't listen to me so I didn't go back the following year. I still plan to try out for high school cheerleading, though!"

That's not such an inspirational story.

"My mother wants me to be famous one day," Madison continues, "so my parents put me in acting classes on the weekends. I've had small roles in community theater shows. It means I hang out with adults a lot of the time and don't get to spend much time with my friends, but I guess I don't mind because I'm learning the craft of acting and it will look good on my résumé if my dad ever lets me audition for commercials, which he won't yet!"

Hmmm. That story doesn't sound any better.

Madison keeps going. "As many of you know, I have won the Friendship Community School penmanship competition almost every year since we learned how to write."

Okay, well, I guess that's pretty cool, if anybody wrote things down on paper anymore. If I didn't hate—I mean, *strongly dislike*—Madison so much, I might be happy for her and all her accomplishments. But I'm not.

"If you want to accomplish your goals, you have to be organized," Madison is saying. Then, out of nowhere, there's a sound—like my stomach gurgling when I'm really hungry, or a stretching cat with laryngitis meowing long and loud.

Everyone kind of looks at each other, like *What was that?* But no one says anything. Madison continues, saying, "I have goals for each day, each week, even each hour." Then we hear it.

FARRRRRRRRRRT!

Sam glances at me. I feel like everything around us has stopped, including Earth turning on its axis.

I look at Madison carefully. She has a really uncomfortable look on her face. Her eyes are big and she moves just a little bit, like her butt is clenching in her tight jeans.

This has got to be it! Sam and I look at each other in shock and unbelievable happiness. At least part of our hex is working! Uncle Arnie is right. My dad is wrong. Voodoo is totally real and my life is better already because I'm feeling so happy!

Madison forces a sick-looking smile and keeps going. "I have a bulletin board at home with cards of things I want to get done. I also put up pictures of things I like and places I want to go someday, which help inspire me. . . ."

FARRRRRRRRRRRT! This one is longer and louder, and it's even more obvious where it came from. Samantha and I are too shocked to laugh, though everyone else is starting to.

"Kids, calm down. Let Madison finish her presentation," Roberta says, but she can't help herself from making a face because now she's *smelling* something really bad like the rest of us are. It's a cross between a dead skunk on the side of the road and a bologna sandwich that's been left out on the counter until it's green around the edges.

"Roberta, could I . . . come back another day? I don't . . . feel well," Madison says, as we all hear the next FARRRRRRRRRRRRRRT! Now bursts of laughter start popping like firecrackers out of people's mouths, even if they're trying to hold it in.

Madison doesn't run out the door—she's too cool for that—but her feet move very quickly and I can tell her body is extremely stressed . . . especially her butt cheeks. Roberta watches her go, then turns to us, looking confused. I guess she doesn't know what we should do now that our special presentation has skittered away, leaving nothing behind but a bad smell hanging in the air. I almost feel sorry for her.

But not quite.

"Quiet down, everybody!" Roberta shouts, then tells us to grab some index cards and markers and make the kinds of cards Madison talked about. She says she'll be right back, and then she runs out the door, looking like she's tightening up a smile. After she's gone for a few seconds, the class finally explodes with the laughter they've all been holding back.

When it calms down a little, Samantha pipes up, "That was the best presentation ever!" That makes everyone crack up again. People nod in agreement and start saying the same kinds of things to each other. For the tiniest second, it feels like we're part of the crowd.

Samantha and I don't have to talk; I know what we're both thinking.

Is this the beginning of being popular?

11

When I get home from school, I run down the hallway to my room, sort of hearing Dad shout that I should take Toby on a walk around the lake. "I will!" I yell back, but first I get the voodoo box from under my bed. I open it and the voodoo doll is lying right where I left him, exactly the same, but it almost looks like he's grinning bigger than usual. I pull him out and dance around my room, thanking him (inside my head, not out loud) for making the charm work on Madison today. Lying on the floor, I gently and carefully put him back and slide the box where it belongs— way under the bed, far from nosy people like Terri.

"Terri's coming over for dinner tonight," Dad says, his voice getting closer along with his footsteps. When I look up, he's standing in my doorway.

"Okay," I say. Even this news can't upset me too much, not right now. I feel like I'm filled with helium and could float to the ceiling. I keep remembering the moment Samantha made her little comment and everyone cracked up. For one instant, it felt like popularity.

"Good, I'm glad you think so," Dad says. "What are you doing down there? Chasing dust bunnies?"

"Ha ha, yeah." I stand up and dust my jeans off. "No, I—um—thought Toby's leash might be under there."

"It's in the front hallway, where it always is," Dad says. "Come on, I'll help you get it on him." When he turns around, I follow him, almost skipping down the hall.

Dad puts the leash around Toby's neck as I hold him in place. I pet his long red fur and let him lick my face and neck, telling him what a good boy he is.

When I head out the door, Dad tells me, "Get home way after dark, talk to lots of strangers, and don't call if there's an emergency." That's his way of being hilarious. He can actually see me from the kitchen window as long as I only walk two blocks and turn around. He even got me a phone when we moved to California. He says it's for safety, but I'm glad because all the kids here have them. So far he and Samantha are the only people I've ever called or texted, but that's definitely going to change when I'm popular.

Toby seems as happy as I am as he barks at the birds flying above us. We cross our street at the corner after I look both ways; then we're on the sidewalk by the lake. It's got little tiny waves because there's a cool breeze, and the sun is making diamond-looking sparkles on top. Maybe these are the kinds of things Mom said are magical. And today, after seeing what I saw, hearing what I heard, and smelling what I smelled, it feels like magic might be possible. I definitely know voodoo is. I mean, Sam and I aren't quite popular *yet,* but there's only so much that a Positive Happy Voodoo Doll can do in a day.

Back at the house, I can hear Dad and Terri talking and laughing in the kitchen. I don't want to see Terri yet, so I let go of Toby with his leash on and head straight back to my bedroom. Dad hears me and says loudly, "Wash your hands and get ready for a sumptuous repast!" I guess he means dinner. He's showing off by using big words for Terri—and by asking me to wash my hands. I don't usually do that; why would I today? I run my hands under some water in the bathroom sink so he'll hear the water, but I don't use any soap.

There aren't any towels in the bathroom, so I go to my room and dry my hands on my comforter. As I'm walking out the door, I stop to check on Millie and Marty. But something is wrong.

Marty isn't moving. I poke her a little with my finger and try to tempt her appetite with a piece of old apple, but I know what's going on. Marty, as they say on TV shows, "is gone."

I take an extra close look at Millie and he's doing fine, squirming around in the grass acting like there's nothing wrong. Maybe those two weren't very close.

I close my eyes tightly and make my mouth hard so I won't cry. I don't know exactly why I'm feeling like this. Marty was just a millipede, a little wormlike creature. She wasn't energetic and fun like Toby, or fluffy and adorable like a bunny or a guinea pig, but she was still my pet and I took care of her like I was supposed to. I walk to the kitchen, where Dad and Terri are in the middle of making dinner. He's got garlic sizzling in a pan and she's slicing celery as some kind of old-timey music from the eighties plays in the background.

"Dad," I say real seriously. They don't hear because they're trying to figure out the lyrics from some song about balloons.

"Dad," I say louder, and they both turn. "Marty died."

Terri looks worried. "Who's Marty? Someone you know?"

"My millipede," I say.

"Well, it's a good thing we bought two!" Dad makes it sound like a joke, but it's not very funny. Terri must not think so either, because she says "Bradley!" in a kind of harsh way.

"Is the other one okay?" Dad asks, his voice softer now.

"Yes. But I'm sad. I don't know why; I can't help it."

Terri puts down her knife and wipes her hands on a rag on the counter. "Cleo, do you want to get Marty and do something nice for him?" she asks. I blink my eyes hard and nod. I don't bother to tell her that Marty is—or was—a girl. "Why don't we give him a proper funeral and say a few things on his behalf?" she says. "You could wrap Marty up in a little piece of paper or material or something. Carry him really carefully to the backyard. I'll get a shovel from your dad, and we can dig a hole and say goodbye." Normally I'd be mad that she's being so friendly, but I'm too sad to be mad. We agree to meet in a few minutes.

I look around in my underwear drawer and find a soft, silky scarf that my mom wore when I was a baby. It has little Eiffel Towers and French poodles on it, and Dad told me she thought it would be neat for me to wear when I grew up and traveled the world.

I pick up Marty gently and wrap her in the scarf. I walk past Dad in the kitchen. He's still working on dinner. "You okay, Cleo?" he asks. I nod without saying anything. "Do you want me to come outside too?"

"No. Terri and I will do it." I don't want too many people around.

In the yard, I can't believe what I see. There's a candle flickering on the grass and Terri is finishing digging a hole. Marty won't take up much room, so it didn't have to be too deep.

I hold out the scarf that's holding Marty.

"Is that him?" Terri asks.

"Her," I say. "I found out she was a girl after I named her."

"Well, Marty's a good name for a girl too." Terri looks down at the hole, with the light from the candle making patterns over it. "Why don't you gently put her in the ground?"

I take a deep breath and get down on my knees. I gently

slide Marty out of the scarf and into the hole. I look up at Terri. "Do you want to say anything?" she asks.

"Just that I loved her, I guess." I can barely get the words out because I'm trying not to cry, but the tears are falling no matter what my brain is telling my eyes.

"It's okay." Terri holds out her hand and helps me stand up. I could have done it myself, but it's still a nice gesture. "I'll say something if that's okay," she says. I nod, and she looks down at the hole in the ground. "Marty, I'm a little scared of creepy-crawly animals, but I know that you were a great one because Cleo loved you. I'm sorry I screamed when I first met you. . . ."

"That was Millie," I tell her.

"I'm sorry I screamed when I first met your friend, but when I held you—or your friend—today, I realized there is nothing to be afraid of."

At that moment, I feel a hotness in my feet that moves up through my whole body like a lightning bolt in a thunderstorm. "What are you talking about?" I ask. My face feels like it just caught on fire. "You *held* Marty? When?"

Terri suddenly has a worried look on her face. "Today," she says. "When you were walking your dog."

"His name's Toby!" I say angrily. I know that's not important right now, but it matters to me. "What did you do to her? What did you do to Marty?"

"Cleo, I didn't do anything. Your dad brought me into your room. . . ."

"Into my *room*?" What was Terri doing in my room? Why is she with my dad? Why is she forcing herself into our lives when we're fine by ourselves?

"Well, in the doorway. He didn't want me to be so scared of the millipedes, so he put one of them on my hand. It only crawled on my hand for a second; nothing happened. It was—"

"*She* was! Marty was a *she*!" I'm yelling now and I'm crying too, but now I don't care because these tears are mean, angry ones, not sad ones that I don't understand. I run into the house and through the kitchen. Dad obviously hasn't heard anything; he's still singing and slicing and cooking. "She killed my millipede!" I stomp through and keep going. "Your *girlfriend* killed Marty! I hope you're happy!"

I run to my room, slam the door shut, and throw myself onto my bed, crying loud and hard and wiping my wet face on my bed. After a few minutes I tire myself out and just lie there breathing.

Finally I sit up. I'm sick to my stomach and scared to check on Millie. But I know I have to. My feet feel like there are ten-pound weights on them, but I pull them across the floor anyway. I look into Millie and Marty's—now only Millie's—terrarium.

Everything is fine.

I pull up my chair and watch him for a while. He slides through the dirt and bark and nibbles a little bit on a brown piece of banana. He looks lonely.

I have to listen hard to hear what's happening down the hall in the kitchen. The music is off and I can hear Dad's and Terri's voices, but I can't tell what they're saying. Then I decide I don't care and I lie back in bed, looking at the ceiling.

I must fall asleep for a little while, because the next thing I hear is a light knock at my door.

I sit right up. "What?" I ask angrily.

"Can I come in?" Dad asks.

"Are you alone?"

"Yes, Terri went home."

"Good."

"So can I come in?" he asks again.

"Yeah, I guess." I'd like to make him wait, but he's going to get in sooner or later.

Dad opens the door but doesn't come in too far. "Listen. I'm really sorry about what happened to Marty."

"It's not your fault. It's hers."

Dad takes a step closer to me. "Cleo, I know how mad you are right now, but that is not true. Terri didn't do anything. Marty crawled on her hand for a couple of seconds. No different from how you and I have played with her. It's no one's fault. Do you understand that?"

I start to cry. "But why? Why did Terri have to touch her? Why did Marty have to die?"

Dad comes closer and sits on the floor by my bed. "It

happens, Cleo. Sometimes pets die when you least expect it. Maybe it was just her time."

"But millipedes have a life span of five to seven or seven to ten years, depending on what website you look at," I tell him, sniffling in between the words.

"That's the problem, Cleo," Dad says. "You don't know when it's going to happen, and lots of times there's no reason at all."

"But I hate it." I pause. "I mean, I don't like it."

Dad smiles a little. "No, it's okay to hate it, Cleo. It's really hard. The only thing you can do is keep living your life the best you can, and make sure that when that person looks down at you from heaven, she's proud."

"You mean millipede," I say.

"Yes. I mean millipede." Dad has little tears in his eyes, just around the edges.

I didn't know he liked Marty that much.

12

The first thing I do in the morning is go to the terrarium and make sure Millie is alive. When I see him crawling around like normal, I run to the kitchen to pick out the rottenest piece of banana we have so he can eat an awesome feast while I'm at school.

"You feel all right after last night?" Dad asks.

"Yeah," I say. "At least Millie's doing okay."

I throw my clothes on—not even caring if my socks match—and I walk out back. I don't see the gravesite at first because there are lots of patches of dirt in between the grassy spots of our yard. Then I notice a big rock that I've never seen before. I walk over to it, thinking about Marty—remembering the way she liked rotten apple better than banana, and how she felt cool and tickly when she crawled on my arm.

As I get closer I see that underneath the big rock are a bunch of smaller ones spelling out a word.

LOVE.

I don't know who did it. Dad? Terri? Mom up in heaven? Magic?

I don't know, but I like that it's there.

When I see Sam at school, I don't tell her about last night. She never even met Marty, and I don't want to ruin the good feeling she has from Madison's awesome embarrassment. Pretty soon my sadness goes away a little bit, because everywhere I go, I'm hearing stories of Madison's presentation and its spectacular, stinky twist.

"Were you really there?" a seventh-grade girl asks me in the bathroom. I nod. "That must've been so funny."

"It was," I say, but I can't think of anything to add because I'm so surprised a stranger is talking to me.

"Excellent. Well, see you around," she says, and heads out.

Wow. I stand there, staring at the bathroom door. Could this be it? Is the second part of our hex coming "to fruition" already?

Is this what being popular feels like? People you don't know talk to you and say "see you around" like they actually *want* to see you around? During our outdoor break, I almost feel like a celebrity as I stroll proudly across the courtyard to the jungle gym. Sam's already there and she says the same kind of thing happened to her, except it was a boy who's not in Focus! but wished he was. That's definitely the first time I've heard of anyone wanting to be in Focus! I think we actually might be popular!

Out of nowhere, Scabby Larry comes up and sits down next to us. "How cool was Focus! class yesterday?" he says.

"Totally cool!" I reply. It's hard not to be happy, and even though it's only Scabby Larry, I can't remember another time when anyone has joined me and Samantha during outdoor break, unless it's Madison and her friends making fun of us.

"Could it have been something she ate?" Scabby Larry wonders out loud. "I can't imagine Madison eating a lot of beans. What else makes you fart?"

"What makes you think Cleo and I want to sit here and talk to you about farts?" Samantha asks.

"Just making conversation."

"Well, maybe you should converse with other Focus! kids," Samantha suggests. "We're busy."

"Okay," Scabby Larry says, standing up. "Just thought it'd be fun to talk about." Then he walks away.

"Why'd you do that?" I ask.

Samantha leans in, looking up at me through her curly bangs. "Remember what I told you about Scabby Larry before? If we're going to be popular, we have to be careful about who we talk to."

"But other kids in Focus! talk to him."

"Other kids in Focus! are *not* cool," Samantha tells me.

"Well, we're not that cool either," I say. She's my best friend; I have to be honest.

"We're cool in our own way, and people are starting to realize it," Samantha says. "In *our* way, we're the coolest people in school."

"In *our* way, we're the coolest people in Los Angeles!" I say. I'm stretching the truth a bit, because LA has movie actors and rock stars and people who are famous for no reason, but even they're not cool in *our* way.

"In *our* way, we're the coolest people on Earth!" Sam says.

We both laugh; then the bell rings and we head to science class, where Kevin announces it's time for two students to do their presentations. I can breathe easy because mine's not until next week, but Kylie Mae has bad luck, probably for the first time in her life, and has to go first. Hers is about photosynthesis, which is how plants turn carbon dioxide into oxygen. That's all I learn, though, because she talks real quietly and doesn't have any fun stuff to show—no drawings or pictures or real plants or anything. I look for some kind of energy or enthusiasm in those empty eyes of hers, but I don't see anything. So I snooze and daydream. But I perk up when I hear who's going next.

Madison Paddington!

If I had farted like her in front of people (even Focus!

people), I would have asked Kevin if I could go last—or do my presentation for him after school, without anyone watching. But as Madison gets out of her chair and walks to the front, I don't see any fear on her face. If I didn't *not like* her so much, I might even be impressed.

She stands next to our classroom's TV and turns to us. "As many of you know," she begins, "my father is a movie producer, and twelve years ago one of his movies even won a People's Choice Award."

I start to get excited—not because her dad won an award, big whoop—but because it sounds like we'll be watching a movie. I'm going to be well rested after this science class for sure!

"He's currently producing a science fiction movie that's going to be released next summer, and he's letting me show you some clips so I can tell you what's realistic scientifically and what's not."

Hmmm. I don't want to give Madison too much credit, but this sounds sort of interesting. She turns on the TV and Kevin turns off the lights. The first movie scene shows a robot acting like a butler in a futuristic house that's all white and clean with almost nothing in it. "Believe it or not," Madison says, "this kind of robot already exists. They can't do everything, but they can perform simple household tasks. People in Japan use them like expensive toys. . . ."

All of a sudden I feel something poking at my butt—a little poke, like from a toothpick. I reach my hand down, and it's a piece of folded-up paper from Sam, who's sitting behind me. I'm a little annoyed because Madison's presentation is actually kind of cool. But I open up the paper and read it.

Next hex? it says.

I turn around, but Sam makes a hissing noise so I turn back toward the front. I sneak a pencil out of my desk, but I don't know what to write so I tap it a couple of times. Our hex worked perfectly and we're on the road to being popular. There isn't anything else I want.

Finally I stop tapping my pencil and write: *Not sure. What could be better than this?*

Without turning my body too much, I place the paper on Sam's desk behind me.

Meanwhile, there's a spaceship on the screen and Madison is talking about how technology is getting closer to science fiction every day. "But right now, the fastest vehicle ever was the Apollo Ten rocket, which went almost twenty-five thousand miles per hour. . . ."

Sam's piece of paper pokes at my butt again. I grab it. It says: *Fix Madison!*

"Fix" Madison? What exactly does that mean? If Sam wants to fix Madison, it means she's broken. How is she broken? I tap my pencil as I think. I guess she's broken . . . because she's mean. So I write back: *How? Make her nicer?* This time I hold the paper in my hand down by my side. Sam takes it from me and writes her next note. *Let's do it!*

I'm scribbling *Okay!* when the lights suddenly go on. But Madison's presentation isn't over.

"Madison, take your seat," Kevin says, walking over to the TV and pausing the picture on the screen. Then he looks at me and Sam. "What are you two doing?"

Neither of us answers at first. It's completely quiet in the room for what feels like forever. Finally Sam says, "Watching the movie."

"And what have you learned?" Kevin asks.

We're both quiet again. I try to answer this one. "Ummm . . . that I'd like a robot butler."

A couple of people laugh. Madison leans over toward her friends and mouths the word "Lazy." Now I'm sorry that I liked her presentation even for a second.

"Were you two passing notes?" Kevin asks.

"No," I answer quickly. "I was putting my gum away because I remembered you don't like gum in class." I pretend to take chewing gum out of my mouth and put it in the paper, and I fold it up real small. Then I shove it in the front of my pants because these pants are more like leggings and don't have any pockets.

"Ewww, weird!" Madison squeals. "I guess they don't have trash cans in *Ohio*!" She giggles at her hilarious comment and a few other people laugh.

Oh well, Sam and I were popular for about five hours and thirteen minutes, but that's more popularity than I've ever had before. It was good while it lasted, but I guess now it's time to go back to normal. . . .

Then a fantastic thing happens.

A fart sound!

It's not a real fart; it's just someone making the noise with their mouth. But more people laugh at this than at what Madison said.

Kevin gives up. "Quiet down, everybody! Let's get back to Madison's presentation," he says. "And I expect everyone to pay attention." Then, before he unpauses the screen, there's another fake fart like the first one. It sounds like a boy's voice. I glance over at Scabby Larry. From the look on his face I know right away it was him. I smile. And I don't even listen to the rest of the presentation because I'm too busy thinking about how if Sam and I succeed in making Madison nice, I'm going to be even happier than I am now.

13

Friday after school, I check my email. I know it's old-fashioned and nobody uses it much anymore, but I'm always hoping for an update from the *Millipede Enthusiast* newsletter I signed up for. It's only come once so far, though. I guess there's not that much millipede news.

But today there's an email that surprises me. The sender's address is *ArnoldJuju* so I know before I even click that it's got to be Uncle Arnie.

And it sure is!

There isn't any message at all. It's just a picture of him with his eyes and mouth wide open. He's got some hair shooting out of his ears now, and he's holding a piece of paper next to his face.

I lean in and squint so I can read the paper, and as soon as I do, I run down the hallway and tell Dad that Sam needs to come over *inmediatamente*!

"What are you talking about?" Dad asks, scrunched over his computer.

"*Inmediatamente* means 'immediately' in Spanish," I tell him.

"Yeah, I could guess that."

"Then why did you ask?" He gives me a look like I'm irritating him, so I get down to business. "Can Sam come over, like, *pronto*?" Then I explain, "*Pronto* means 'soon' in Spanish."

"I get it, I get it," he says. He stands up and stretches. "But I'm supposed to have Terri over for dinner tonight, and you two should spend some time together. Can't we ask Sam over tomorrow or Sunday?"

"No, we can't!" It's very important that Sam come over *now*, because what I saw in Uncle Arnie's email is going to make our next hex even more super-awesomely-wonderful than our last one. But of course I can't tell Dad *that*. "Sam and her mom are going away tomorrow morning, so if I don't see her tonight I won't see her until Monday, and I really, really need to see her tonight."

"Weren't you together all day at school?"

Ugh! Dads don't understand anything!

"Come on, Dad. We can make dinner for Sam and her mom, and I'll help cook and I'll clean up and even though I'm still extremely depressed about Marty, I'll be totally nice to Terri the next time I see her. I bet she'd love to see you tomorrow."

I beg and beg, then beg a little bit more, and finally he calls Sam's mom. I only hear his end of the conversation, but I can tell Paige is telling him what I already know—that they're going to Mexico for the weekend. It sounds glamorous, but Samantha says it's only a couple hours' drive. Her mom goes to a spa on the beach while Sam visits her dad.

I look at Dad really hard, like my staring could make Sam come over. I've never had a friend like Samantha, ever— someone I can joke *and* talk about serious things with, and hang out with for hours, and share special secrets with like voodoo. I thought I had a good friend back in Ohio—Jane Anne—but when fourth grade turned into fifth, she became a "cool" girl and ignored me after that. So in a way, I wasn't totally bummed when Dad and I moved to California.

On the phone Dad is saying, "Are you sure that's okay, Paige? We don't want to get in the way of your packing or anything." It sounds like Paige is saying yes! "Okay, then, we'll see you around seven."

Dad clicks the phone off and I cheer and jump up and down. "Thank you!" I shout, then give him a big hug.

"You're very welcome," he says, grumbling. "But you owe me one."

He starts to dial another number as I shout, "I owe you one, two, three, and four. I owe you everything, Dad! I owe you my life."

"Okay, that's enough." He walks away from me into the kitchen so he can cancel his plans with Terri.

I'm glad. I mean, I kind of understand that she didn't kill Marty, and I *will* try to be nice to her next time like I promised, but that doesn't mean I like her. Dad should like Samantha's mom instead. That way I'd get to spend lots more time with Sam. So after he's off the phone with Terri, I suggest real casually that he make his best, most tasty homemade meal—chicken with rice and bacon green beans. And when I smell bacon sizzling on the stove at 6:30, I know he agreed.

I get another idea when I look at our scratched and scruffy kitchen table with old, old stains and tiny crumbs that never quite disappear. "Hey, Dad, do we have a tablecloth?"

"Ummm, I don't know," he says. "Look in the closet with the towels and blankets."

I look, but the best thing I find is a sheet with little flowers on it. I fold it a few times and put it on the table, smoothing it out to look nice.

"That looks good," Dad says. "We'll have to buy a real tablecloth sometime." He's come up with a plan for the night—he says we'll all eat dinner together and then we kids can play afterward. I don't bother correcting Dad when he says "play." The voodoo instructions say that "a voodoo doll is not a toy," and we know that now. We are not planning to *play* at all.

When the doorbell rings, Toby goes crazy barking and jumping. Inside I'm as excited as he is, but I try to act like a popular kid would and take my time getting to the door. It's hard, though, because I'd really rather run!

Samantha's in the clothes she wore to school and her mom is wearing a silky blouse and sparkly necklaces that hang low between her boobs. Her super-shiny black hair is long instead of pulled back, and her lipstick is very red. Terri barely wears any makeup and always dresses casual like us. How could Dad *not* like Sam's mom more?

Toby jumps up on her, and there's nothing she can do because she has a bottle of wine in one hand and a small bag from a fancy store in the other. She's saying things like "Nice dog, cute dog," but it doesn't look like she likes him for real. Classy ladies like her probably aren't dog people. Dad runs in from the kitchen, yelling, "Toby! Get down!" and grabs him by the collar. "I'm sorry, Paige; he's excited. He's not used to visitors."

"He's used to Terri," I say; then I realize I probably shouldn't mention Terri at all.

"Who's Terry?" Samantha's mom asks. "A handyman?"

"No, just a friend of theirs," Sam tells her. It's great how fast she thinks of stuff.

It's quiet for a second; then Dad invites Paige and Samantha into the kitchen. "Dinner's almost ready, so why don't you girls stay here with us?" Dad says. Samantha and I groan.

"Oh, is it so terrible to hang out with your parents?" Paige asks, and I wonder if Sam likes the sound of "your parents" as much as I do. We sit down at the table while Paige hands Dad the bottle of wine and the fancy bag. There are two candles inside. "I told Mom that it'd be nice to have candles on the table," Samantha tells me. Usually we eat with a bright light shining down on us, but when Paige lights the candles, the room looks classier—like an expensive restaurant where they serve filet mignon.

Samantha and I talk about school things (yawn) that we don't mind the adults overhearing while Paige leans against our kitchen counter drinking a glass of yellow wine and watching Dad finish making dinner. Soon we're sitting around the table all lovely and proper like a regular family. There's not much noise aside from chewing, and Toby's whimpering since no one is feeding him.

"Bradley, these green beans are scrumptious!" Samantha's mom says suddenly. I don't know why, though. Usually they're pretty yummy, but tonight they're too squishy on the inside and too black and crunchy on the outside.

Dad must like hearing it, because he tells her all about his recipe. I see Samantha's face in the candlelight across the table. She raises her eyebrows at me as she pops a green bean into her mouth, smiling as she chews.

We let the adults keep talking until we clean our plates. Then I tell Dad, "We're done!"

"Thanks, it was delicious, Mr. Nelson," Sam says.

"Well, thank you, Sam," Dad says, looking proud. "Cleo, you and Samantha can go to your room if you'd like."

"But I told you I'd help with the dishes." If I'm not honest about it now, I'm sure a different, ickier chore will come back to bite me in the butt later, like cleaning the bathtub or pulling hair out of the sink.

"Don't worry about it; I'll do them later," Dad says. Shock and happiness zip through my body. I'm about to say thanks and give him a hug, but Sam's mom interrupts.

"Oh, I'll help you with them, Bradley," she says. "You did a lot of work tonight."

"You're dressed a little too nice to be washing dishes," Dad says. So he must be attracted to the way she looks! Maybe he *does* like her!

"Okay, we're gonna go!" I say, and make a run for it.

Samantha and I rush down the hallway and lock the door to my room. "What is that smell?" she asks.

"My millipede! For science class!" I say proudly. I pick up the terrarium from my desk and show her how I decorated it, with all its extra twigs and grass.

"It's kinda gross," she says, her nose all crinkled up. "I thought you said they were cute. This looks like a fat worm."

"Oh, they're super cute when you get to know them," I tell her.

"Them?" she asks. "I only see one."

"Oh yeah. I used to have two, but one died. She's buried in the backyard with a gravestone and everything."

"That's too bad," says Sam. "Was it sad?"

"Yeah, pretty sad."

"You should have texted me. I could've tried to make you laugh or sent you a funny video or something."

"That would've been nice," I say. "Thanks, Sam."

"At least you still have one."

"Yeah, that's good, I guess." And what's even better is having a friend like Samantha. She and I don't have to agree on everything, and we're still friends. And I know she'll like millipedes once she spends more time with Millie.

We're quiet for a second; then Sam brings our focus back to the most important matter of the night. "We'd better hurry up and do our hex before my mom decides that I have to go to bed at 8:30."

"But it's Friday!"

"I know! But we're leaving for Rosarito early in the morning and Mom likes having a *sched-u-le*." She says "schedule" in a snooty accent, like her mom might say it.

"Don't worry, they're drinking wine! Adults lose track of time when they drink wine." I feel pretty grown up because I know things like this.

"Why do you think I told my mom to bring some?" says Samantha, and I realize she's pretty grown up too. As I'm sliding under my bed to get the voodoo doll, I hear her say, "What would happen if your dad and my mom liked each other?"

I grab the box from in between some old Lego and a pile of dusty Toby fuzz and come back out quickly. "I was thinking about that too!" I say. "It'd be great!"

"Well, not as great as doing hexes . . ."

"But pretty great!" I say.

"If they started dating, there'd be lots more nights like this. We'd all have dinner together all the time! And not just at home!" Sam's talking almost as fast as I do. "We'd go to restaurants, and movies, and other fun places. . . ."

I jump in. "And if she became his girlfriend and not just a girl-who's-a-friend, we could go on weekend trips and vacations together." I'm already picturing us on the beach in warm, sunny Mexico, even though I've never been there and I don't know what Mexico looks like. I'm picturing a California beach but with tacos and sombreros.

"Then, if they got really serious—" Sam starts to say, and I cut her off because the idea is too exciting to hold in.

"They'd get married!" I shout.

"We'd be sisters!" Sam shouts back.

"We would live together! Like, in the same room!"

"And we could get bunk beds!" Sam says, and I love that idea, though I'd want the bottom bunk because I'd be afraid of falling down the ladder if I had to get up to go to the bathroom in the middle of the night. I don't bother saying that now, because as much as I want my dad and her mom to get married, it's probably a long way off.

Plus, there's something more important to think about right now.

A hex.

14

I hold up the voodoo box to build the excitement. I open it and lift the doll over my head with a dramatic wave of my arms, singing, "Bom-bom-BOMMMMM!" like in a preview for an action movie.

Sam does not appear impressed. Her mind is on something else, I can tell.

"I wonder if there's a way to make this charm work even better," she says. "The farts were awesome, but what if we could do something . . ."

"Bigger?" I suggest, knowing that the email from Uncle Arnie is going to help us do exactly that.

"Yeah! Something that would go down in the history of Friendship Community School."

"Well, I've got something huge to show you! My uncle sent me an email. It's sort of a recipe—"

"A recipe for what?" Samantha cuts me off. She always likes to know things right away. No waiting for Sam.

"To make your hex better," I tell her. Without asking, she leans over and turns on my computer. Computers are pretty private things, but when we're sisters we'll share things all the time, so I guess it's no big deal.

"Well, that sounds interesting." Sam goes straight to my email in-box and clicks on the message from Uncle Arnie. It's the first time she's seen him, and she jumps back from the computer. "Whoa! Is that your uncle?" Sam asks. "He looks crazy."

I'm getting used to Uncle Arnie, but to a person seeing him for the first time, I would have to agree.

"Is that the recipe?" Sam asks, pointing at the paper. I nod. "Why did he send a picture of it instead of typing it out?"

I sigh. "With Uncle Arnie, who knows?"

"So what does it say?"

I blow up the photo so we can read it more clearly. The instructions are in an old-fashioned-looking font.

Increase the strength and vibrancy of your hex quickly and easily with three simple ingredients! Take your Positive Happy Voodoo Doll and dip it in vinegar, wheatgrass juice, or an equally unpleasant liquid. Roll your doll in cinnamon

and steel-cut oats. Place your doll back in its box and hide it in darkness until your spell comes to fruition. Have fun hexing!

"So, are we trying it?" I ask Sam.

"Of course we're trying it! Do you have any of that stuff?"

"Probably. Or something close." I'm already up on my feet and heading toward my door. "Let's go."

Sam and I walk down the hallway toward the kitchen. Dad and Sam's mom are sitting in their same seats at the table, not saying anything. It's weird that it's so quiet. If Terri were here, there would probably be some music on, and she and Dad would be singing or laughing. But those are the kinds of things friends do. Dad and Paige are acting more like adults. Maybe that's a good sign. Maybe when you're busy falling in love, you don't have to talk too much.

"Hey, Dad, do we have any vinegar?" I ask. They both look startled by the interruption.

"That's a strange dessert," Dad says, and looks at Paige. She laughs loudly, but it sounds sort of fake. If Dad keeps saying dumb things like that, she's never going to like him.

"Ummm, no, it's not for dessert, it's for—ummm . . ."

Sam jumps in with, "Our science experiments!"

"Oh, great," Dad says. "I'm not sure, but check in the cabinets over by the fridge."

"Near the cinnamon?" Sam asks.

"What kind of experiment *is* this?" Dad asks, but I say I'll tell him some other time. Now I'm on the hunt as Sam watches. I find the cinnamon easily because I love cinnamon toast on the weekends. I don't know exactly what steel-cut oats are, but on our breakfast shelf are packets of oatmeal, the kind where you add hot water and suddenly have a meal. I'm sure that's close enough. I grab one of those and bury my head farther into the cabinet. I push things around and knock over a few items, but I don't see any bottles of vinegar or anything else unpleasant-tasting.

When I turn around to tell Sam, I can't believe what I see.

She's holding an open bottle of wine (this one's red, not yellow like pee) and pouring some of it into a cup! I look at her in shock, but she makes a "shhh" mouth at me. She quietly puts the bottle back on the kitchen counter and holds the cup down low. "I think we've got everything we need," she whispers, keeping her back to her mom and my dad.

Now we have to walk right past them with Samantha holding wine. But for once I get a brilliant idea. Toby is sitting under the table between Dad and Paige, waiting for scraps of food that he doesn't realize are already in the trash.

"Toby, Toby, Toby!" I shout, and he jumps up instantly, barking back at me. He tries to run but he can't get through the adults' legs that are like prison bars between us.

"Oh, Cleo, why did you get him all riled up?" Dad asks. He and Paige both have their attention on the dog pushing against their legs under the table as Samantha slips past holding the wine.

"Sorry, Dad. He looked bored."

"Hush, doggy, hush," Sam's mom is saying to Toby, but that's not a command he understands. We'll have to turn her into a dog person when she joins our family.

Sam's already out of the dining room and is zooming down the hallway to my bedroom. I follow her, holding the oatmeal packet and cinnamon tin, saying "sorry" again to Dad as I go.

When I get to my room, I close the door behind me, relieved but laughing. When Sam and I are sisters, we'll sneak around and make up pranks and do this kind of stuff all the time.

"That was fun!" Sam says.

"I can't believe you poured their wine!"

She takes a big sniff of it. "Well, it smells unpleasant, like your uncle wanted. Come on, let's get hexing before our parents decide they're done."

Our parents. It definitely sounds nice.

I find my science notebook and fish out the V.I.H.—very

important hair—from the plastic folder. I wind the real hair around the yarn hair and look at the doll. I feel bad that he's going to be covered in wine and cinnamon and oatmeal, but I pick him up and take him to Sam, who's still holding the wine. The cup is too small to fit the whole doll inside, so I dunk him up to his tutu.

"My turn, my turn," Sam insists. I hand her the doll, dripping some wine on the floor. I grab the closest piece of paper I see. Unfortunately it's one of my unfinished Panda-roo drawings, but it's all I can find, so I place it over the red spots on the floor.

"Hold the doll over the paper," I say as she hands me the cup. She dunks his head and shoulders in, dripping even more wine on my drawing.

"Let's put the other ingredients on your picture and roll it around on there," Sam suggests. Since it already has spots of wine on it, what's the difference if we make an even bigger mess? Dry oatmeal flakes join Pandaroo as he flies around in space; then I add a few dashes of cinnamon "for flavor," I joke. Sam and I each take a turn rolling the doll in the mess, our fingers turning red from the wine.

We leave the doll on the paper and sit on either side of him. Since we hope Madison will say nicer things when her personality changes, Sam decides to put the pin on the doll's mouth. I set my cell phone's timer for five minutes. We don't want to risk concentrating for too short a time when we want this charm to be even bigger and better—and getting Madison to be nice is a major goal. From far down the hallway I hear the sound of dishes being washed and Dad talking to Samantha's mom. Then I remember I need to focus. It's hard to imagine Madison being nice, but I think about how the girl in the bathroom said "see you around." That's all Madison would need to do. No more piggy and clown comments; no more sneering and making faces. I think about how amazing it'll be if this hex works like the last one. Everyone in school will be so excited, and if they ever found out Sam and I were behind it, they'd laugh and joke and be our friends forever. Not that I really *need* any more friends besides Samantha—she's the best—but now that I've experienced over five hours of popularity, I know that a few more friends would be a positive addition to my life.

I realize I need to concentrate more on Madison, and I do. Then the alarm goes off and we're finished. I feel a little uncertain, but when I look at Samantha, her eyes are wide and happy, as if she's saying *"This is going to be awesome."*

The doll is still dripping with wine, so we roll him up in my Pandaroo picture, which is big enough to wrap around him a few times. We put the doll in his box and tuck him away back under my bed. We rush to the bathroom with the cup of wine after glancing down the hallway to make sure no one's coming.

The wine smells like dirt and looks like blood as it goes down the drain. Why would anyone want to drink that? We wash our hands; then I wipe off the sink and we run back to my room to pretend like we've been doing other stuff the whole time. I get Millie out of his terrarium, and though Samantha is nervous at first, she lets him crawl across her arm.

That's when her mom knocks and, without waiting, walks in. She gasps when she sees my wormy buddy crawling up her daughter. "What's that?" she asks, shocked.

"Millipede," we both say.

"His name's Millie. He's for my science project. I'm showing him to the class on Monday," I add, but she doesn't look interested.

"Is that . . . *smell* coming from it?" she asks, her nose all wrinkled.

"No, that's from his food. He eats fruits and vegetables and he likes them best when they're rotted," I tell her.

She takes a breath and then sips from her almost-empty wine glass. "O . . . kay. Well, Sam, please take that . . . *thing* off your body, then go to the bathroom and wash your arm. Thoroughly. I mean it. Use hot water. But don't dawdle. It's way past your bedtime, and mine too. So get your things and come out and thank Mr. Nelson again for the lovely dinner he made us."

"Okay, Mom," Sam replies without whining at all, and heads right to our bathroom.

We all say goodbye at the front door. Paige says how nice it was to see us and gives Dad a hug. Dad looks surprised but hugs her back and says we'll have to do it again soon.

They must be falling in love already!

"Bye, sister," Sam says with a wink.

"Bye, sis," I say. I like the sound of it. A lot.

15

I'm nervous going to school on Monday for a whole bunch of reasons. (1) I didn't practice my science presentation very well at all. I forgot about it all day Saturday and I only did it in my head when I was in bed on Sunday night. Then I fell asleep halfway through. (2) Now that Samantha's mom mentioned it, I've noticed how smelly Millie's box really is. Maybe I should have chosen a lovable animal that would make Madison and her friends say "awww" or "kewwwwt" instead of "ick" and "ugh." (3) I'm worried about the hex. I'm sure it will work. The only question is when. And how?

I walk into the classroom and, as I predicted, my terrarium does not go unnoticed.

"Ewww," sneers Madison. "Did you forget to put on deodorant today, Cleo?"

"I don't *wear* deodorant!" I bark at her, though right away I wish I could take it back. Dad says deodorant is for twelve years old and up, unless I start stinking sooner, which I haven't. But I didn't need to *say* it—out *loud*—to Madison and her friends.

"Oh, we can tell!" Lisa Lee says, grinning at Madison. Kylie Mae, her blue eyes staring at nothing, nods like usual. That's no life.

"It's not me, it's my millipede," I say, holding up the box, but I'm already realizing I'm not going to win this one. Things are back to normal at Friendship Community School. Samantha and I didn't concentrate on how long our popularity would last, and now I'm sure it's over.

Luckily that's when Samantha comes in and stands next to me, straight and proud, glaring at Madison. "Yeah, Cleo's got the coolest millipede in the world and she's going to do a killer presentation today—with lots of other surprises!"

"I'll be surprised if I don't pass out from the smell," Madison says. Then Kevin shouts for us all to sit down, so we don't get to say anything else. I'm glad I have Samantha, though; I never know the right thing to say. Obviously.

When science class starts, Kevin calls on Scabby Larry to go first. He holds up a big piece of cardboard with a black-and-white picture of an old guy on it—a guy who kind of looks like Uncle Arnie. His hair is whiter, but it's fuzzy like Uncle Arnie's and standing straight up. This guy doesn't have Uncle Arnie's scruffy beard, but he does have a mustache. Plus he's sticking his tongue out—something I can definitely picture Uncle Arnie doing.

"This is Albert Einstein," Scabby Larry says. Wow. I know Albert Einstein is a famous old scientist, so I didn't expect him to look like a kook. "You've probably heard of him, but you might not know that he changed the way we look at matter."

Matter, according to Scabby Larry, is really just "stuff," and he says matter never really goes away; it only changes form and becomes something else. Scabby Larry is actually pretty smart and interesting sometimes. I kind of wish Samantha liked him more—maybe he could even be a friend—but I don't think I could ever change her mind about him.

As Scabby Larry continues talking about energy and the speed of light, there's some noise behind me. A chair scrapes on the floor, and I hear a loud, high *woo-woo* squeal. Everyone turns, and Kevin sits up in his seat like my dad does when he's falling asleep watching TV. "What's going on back there?" he asks.

Madison suddenly jumps out of her seat, and her screaming gets higher and louder. What I hear next is something I *do not* want to hear. Madison, her face all scrunched-up and red, screams, "Cleo's worm!"

Now *I* jump out of my seat. Millie's box is on its side! There's dirt and grass on the floor, and Millie is nowhere to be seen! Madison is bouncing around wildly. She could step on Millie and kill him if she's not more careful!

"Stop jumping!" I shout. "He's just a millipede! He's not gonna hurt you!"

"It's gross! Gross, gross, gross!" Madison's batting her hair with both hands. "Did I get it out? Is it out?" she screams to Lisa and Kylie, who both run away to the corner of the room. Then it hits me.

Millie is in Madison's perfect hair! I have no idea how he could have gotten up there, but I don't have time to care about that because I don't want Madison to hurt him! I run to Madison, shouting, "Stop hitting yourself! I'll get him out!"

Madison is breathing heavily and saying "Oh my God" over and over again. I tell her to calm down and I touch a section of her perfect, silky hair, now slightly messy because she was hitting it all around. I hold on to her hair with one hand and gently pick Millie out with the other. "Are you okay?" I ask Millie, using one finger to pet his back so he won't be too upset. He's curled himself up in a ball like millipedes do when they're in trouble.

"Is *it* okay? What the *bleep* are you talking about?" screams Madison. But she doesn't say "bleep." "Kevin! This is *bleepity bleep* ridiculous! *Bleepy* Cleo, and *bleepity bloop blap bleep* your worm!"

I almost start to cry. "He's not a worm, and don't talk about him like that," I say, backing up to take Millie to my seat where he'll be safe. Kevin walks over to Madison, but she doesn't calm down—at all. Now the *bleeps* are coming even faster and longer, and some of the *bleeps* I've never even heard before, but I can tell they're curse words by how everyone in the room is acting. Lisa Lee and Kylie Mae are huddled together in the corner, and I swear their mouths are so wide open that a hummingbird could fly right inside.

Madison is now hopping around like a Mexican jumping bean and batting her hair like Millie's still in there. Her *bleeps* keep coming, but it's not like when I pigged out and Terri said the bad word; Madison is serious and loud and not stopping anytime soon.

Kevin talks to her in a slow, calm voice, puts his hand on her shoulder, and starts guiding her toward the door. "Come on," he says, "let's go call your parents." As they leave, Kevin tells us to put our heads down on our desks and be quiet until he gets back. I bet none of us have done that since we were in kindergarten, but we all do it, slowly, until he and Madison can't be seen anymore. Then everybody's head comes up and they start nervously talking about what just happened. Lisa Lee and Kylie Mae stay in the corner with sour looks on their faces. Some evil henchwomen they are, running away when Madison needed them. Everything is pretty quiet until Scabby Larry says loudly, "That was even better than the farts!" and almost everybody laughs.

I can't laugh, though. What we just saw wasn't funny; it was freaky. Too freaky. My face is hot and I feel sick to my stomach. My body is all tight and nervous, like something even worse is going to happen. Madison definitely wasn't acting nicer—she was doing the opposite, for sure—but I still have a creepy feeling it had something to do with our voodoo.

While Kevin is gone with Madison, kids in class take turns standing guard near the door. As I'm cleaning up the dirt and grass on the floor near Madison's desk, I hear Kylie Mae and Lisa Lee whispering about how they've never heard Madison say any of those words before in their lives, and maybe they don't know her like they thought they did. Samantha's on guard and she hisses to everyone that Kevin's coming back, so we all run to our chairs and put our heads back down on our desks.

Kevin tells us to lift our heads and everyone does, looking like a bunch of little angels in a classroom in heaven. He says there won't be any more presentations today, since our science period is over. We'll start them again tomorrow. "Cleo," he says, "it might be better if you did your presentation tomorrow without your worm."

"It's a millipede!" I'm getting tired of everyone calling Millie a worm, and if I could do my presentation right now I could make them understand.

"Right, right, right. I think it's for the best, though, Cleo. Don't worry, it won't affect your grade. I can see you're very passionate about your millipede and I'm sure your classmates will benefit from a great presentation." He gives me a sympathetic look and a nod, and I feel better. Then

Kevin turns to the class. "Let's get out your history books; we're going to talk about the Emancipation Proclamation today. . . ."

But he's interrupted—by Samantha! "Kevin," she says with a sweetness in her voice that doesn't sound normal. "What happened to Madison?" That's Samantha—not afraid to ask the thing everyone in class wants to know.

Kevin takes a big breath, then tells us that he took Madison to Frederick's office, and Frederick called her parents to take her home. He says she's going to need a "rest" and won't be coming back to school until next week at least. I don't know if that's code for getting in trouble, or what. But later, as we're sitting in our usual spot under the jungle gym, Samantha says, "It looked like a nervous breakdown to me."

"What's that?"

"It's when someone freaks out and they have to go away and spend time with a psychiatrist or psychologist or somebody."

"That sounds serious."

"Maybe," Samantha says. "But who cares? She may not be any nicer, but at least she can't be mean to us when she's not in school. And that's nice for us!"

"So maybe it did work," I say . . . but I'm not happy about it like Sam. "Isn't it weird, though? Madison became a completely different person. That wasn't what we meant to do." Maybe the voodoo doll got things a little confused. But if that's the case, it scares me. We couldn't have predicted that the hex would turn out this way. "It didn't seem like she could control it. And I think we're the ones who did it to her."

"I'm sure we did!" Sam says. "You should be more excited!"

I force a smile and tell her I'll try to be. But inside, I know that's going to be hard.

At the end of the day, Samantha's already gone home and I'm standing on the sidewalk at the edge of school, holding Millie's terrarium and waiting for Dad to pick me up. I'm about to text Sam, just for something to do, when I hear an adult's voice coming toward me—a mean one. "Do you understand how inconvenient this is for me, Madison?" a man says. "I had a meeting with one of my investors in Beverly Hills, and I had to drive all the way out here because your mother insisted we do this together. Do you know what traffic is *like* at this time of day?"

"I'm sorry, Dad." It sounds like Madison's been crying. I hate hearing that kind of sound in *anyone's* voice, even hers.

"You should be!" a lady says. That must be her mother.

They sound close, and I don't want to be seen. I back up slowly, one step at a time, until I'm smashed between two overgrown rosebushes. Even through my T-shirt and jeans, the prickers of the roses poke at me like pointy little voodoo pins.

They're walking quickly as they pass me, Mr. and Mrs.

Paddington in front with Madison trailing behind them. They don't notice me at all. But I can see them perfectly and hear everything they're saying. Madison's mom is wearing a white sweater and short skirt like she should be playing tennis. Her legs are dark orange and don't quite match her face. And her blond hair looks like a marshmallow Peep at Easter—yellow and poofy and perfect, but not in a normal human way like Madison's. She must go to the hairdresser every day.

They get to their big, clean, fancy car, which is parked close by. Too close. I squeeze back even farther into the roses. It hurts, but I turn to my side so there's less of me to see.

"Everything you've wanted, we've provided!" Madison's dad is saying, but it's more like yelling. "What was it first, Heather? Acting lessons?"

"Acting lessons, then ballet, then tap."

"*You* wanted me to do ballet," Madison says.

"Well, what's the point of being in the business if you can't dance *and* act? And you need to sing! She said she was too busy reading! Reading those big giant books she likes. Henry, she wouldn't even *try* singing lessons."

"I didn't want to sing; I wanted to cheerlead!"

"And look how that turned out," her father says.

"*I* had to leave the nail salon to come here!" her mom adds.

"You go there all the time!" says Madison, almost shouting. I doubt shouting is a wise choice, but that's easy for me to say because I'm hiding in the rosebushes, not getting yelled at in the school parking lot.

"Don't talk back to your mother!" Her dad slams his hand on the top of the car. It makes a loud noise, and in that one tiny second my stomach goes from feeling tight and nervous to like I'm going to throw up.

"Henry!" her mom yells. It's quiet for a second; then she says, a little more softly, "We should go."

As her dad opens the car door, Madison stands there. I can't see her face, but I can tell by her shaking shoulders that she's crying. "Come on, Madison, let's go. Don't keep your father waiting." Madison's mom steers her into the backseat and closes the door without even looking to make sure she's all the way in. My dad always looks, even now that I'm not a little kid anymore. "Fingers and toes, fingers and toes," he always says, making sure I'm safe before he closes the door.

Then the fancy car backs up fast and screeches loudly as it zooms forward out of the parking lot.

I stay standing in the rosebushes for a minute. My stomach still feels sick, and if it could feel sad, confused, and scared, it would be that too. I'm almost about to cry when I hear Dad's voice shout out in a jokey way, "Cleo, what in the world are you doing in the bushes?"

"Are you okay?" another voice asks. It's Terri. She's in the front seat next to Dad. I would have rather seen Toby there, but anyone looks better than Henry and Heather Paddington.

I put the terrarium on the ground, run to Dad's open window, and throw myself in to give him a hug. He looks kind of shocked, but he laughs and says, "Good to see you too, Cleo!"

"I love you, Dad!" I say.

"I love you too, kiddo," he says back. "Listen, Terri left work early so we can have an afternoon at the beach. So grab your millipede and let's get going!"

Even with Terri involved, that sounds almost as good as "I love you."

16

Growing up, I could never picture an afternoon when I'd leave school and wind up on the sand looking at the crashing waves of a never-ending ocean. I used to think that everyone in California lived next to the beach, but we're actually a half hour away—even longer when there's traffic. But we're still a lot closer than I was in Ohio!

It's chillier here than it was at school, but so what? It's the beach! Dad and Terri are sitting on a blanket, bundled up in sweatshirts and jackets, talking and taking pictures with their phones. They look cozy, and I think about forcing myself in between them to be rude and annoying, but then I'd just be sitting and staring at the ocean, and that seems boring. So I take off my sneakers and socks and run into the water. It's freezing, but I don't care. I roll up my jeans and walk in a little farther, but when a wave hits me from behind and my butt gets wet, Dad says it's time to get out. As the sun starts going down and the sky gets all cool and pink, I use a stick to draw in the sand. It's too hard to draw one of my animated characters, so I go for something simpler: smiley faces.

Terri looks over. "They don't look very happy," she says.

I look down at the sand and she's right. The smiles are more like straight lines. I guess they're feeling the same way I do about what happened to Madison and what I saw with her parents. But I don't want to talk to Terri about that. Instead I just drag my stick in the sand. "They're not having a very good day," I say.

"Is something wrong?" Dad asks. "Everything okay at school?"

That is a question *way* too complicated to answer, so I just say, "Yeah."

"Hey, wasn't your science presentation today?" Terri asks. "How'd it go?"

Ugh, these are way too many questions for a nice afternoon at the beach. "I'm doing it tomorrow," I tell them. "But everybody saw Millie today, so I'll leave him home."

"So everything's all right?" Dad asks again.

"Yeah, I'm fine. Except that my butt is wet."

"Ah, there are worse things in life," Terri says.

Dad nods. "That's for sure. I, for one, would say it's pretty wonderful out here." Terri leans her head on his shoulder and he pulls her closer to him. They look happy, but after everything that's happened today, I know *I'd* be happier if I were here with a friend like Sam. With Sam, I wouldn't have to say things are fine. Sam knows me better than that.

Back at school, we find out Madison got suspended for at least a week. I feel a little guilty that she's not there, but at least I'm not all tight inside anymore. I don't go to school worried about what she might do or say. I guess this is the feeling that's called relief. That makes me feel even guiltier, though—that I can be so free while Madison is probably trapped at home with her parents. How did things turn out this way?

This voodoo thing is complicated. More complicated than I ever imagined.

My science presentation goes okay without Millie— maybe even a little better since I had an extra night to practice it—but it's nowhere near as interesting without having him to show. I remember to tell everyone about the 6,500 types of millipedes there are in the world, and I like the reaction I get when I describe the bad-smelling "repugnatorial" fluid they can "emit." Some people smile, and I see Scabby Larry say, "Cool!" Kylie Mae and Lisa Lee make faces and maybe cough a few times, but they don't do anything worse.

Sam's presentation is great. She hasn't solved the problem of Earth getting hotter, but she explains it really well. It's sad when she shows photos of adorable polar bears who are losing their homes because glaciers are melting, but I bet that with a little more time, probably by college, Samantha will be able to solve Earth's problem. And I can tell we're going to get As because Kevin says "Excellent job" to both of us.

Later in the week, Samantha's mom calls and I hear her on speakerphone with Dad. She says it's supposed to be "unseasonably hot" this weekend, so I should come over and go swimming in their condo's pool, which is heated all year long. After our cold afternoon at the beach, a warm pool sounds awesome!

On Sunday Dad rings Sam's doorbell, and Paige answers. She has on a really short dress, and I can see through it to a bikini underneath. She's wearing an awful lot of makeup to be going to the pool, but she looks super pretty as usual. Maybe when Sam and I are sisters, Paige will teach us how to be pretty too.

"You look rather nice to be going swimming," Dad says. Sam's mom bats her eyelashes and invites Dad to stay. He says he wishes he could, but he doesn't have a bathing suit with him. "Well, you're wearing shorts. You could get some sun and dunk your toes in," she says.

"Yeah, Dad, stay!" I want to point out that Paige is in a bikini while his *girlfriend* wore a sweatshirt to the beach— understandable because it was cold, but still!

"That sounds great, Paige, but I've got a whole list of

things to do while the girls are with you." He's probably doing stuff with Terri, but he doesn't tell Paige that.

Samantha marches into the living room in a bathing suit, slathered in white sunscreen that's barely rubbed in, carrying two big foam noodles to float on and a bag full of towels and pool toys. "Let's go," she says in a tone that's kind of serious for a fun pool day. "We've got lots to do."

Sam's mom walks us down the stairs to the patio area that all the condos share. The blue of the pool is so sparkly and clean; I would like to *live* in it, except then I guess I'd have to be wet all the time. I jump right in and make a mighty splash. "Come in!" I shout to Sam; then I dive underwater.

When I come up, Sam is standing at the edge of the pool with her hands on her hips. I can't see her mouth because it's in a tight line across her face. "We have things to talk about!" she says. I sigh, loud enough for her to understand that I'd rather be swimming, and get out of the pool. Well, almost. I climb up the ladder halfway and then fall backward into the water with another big splash. I hear Samantha groan and I figure she's going back to her chair under an umbrella.

It's warm enough that I don't bother drying off. "Okay, what?" I ask, changing my attitude. I flash a smile, hoping it's the one that makes me look friendly instead of weird.

"I want to talk about our next hex," she says, raising her

eyebrows. She's got a whole new plan, and it must be pretty juicy because she looks around first to see if anyone's listening. No one is. Her mom is the only other person here, and she's on the other side of the pool reading a magazine under a gigantic hat.

"I have a big idea, and it could change the world and even the universe as we know it!" Sam whispers. "But I don't know if I can talk about it here."

When Samantha talks like this, all focused and determined, it's hard not to let it rub off on you. I know I've been feeling bad about what happened with our last hex, but we don't honestly know *for sure* that we caused Madison's cursing fit. I should at least listen to what Sam has to say.

I put my hands on her shoulders. "Talk about it right now, right here, or you're getting thrown in the pool!"

"Okay. If you insist," Samantha says with a laugh. "For our next hex, I think we should get your dad and my mom together. We need to give them a push. A big one. They're moving pretty slowly on their own."

"Well, that's because Dad likes Terri." Whether I like it or not, it's true.

"Maybe she's the one we could hex then!"

Hmmm. I never thought of anything like that before. If we could get Dad and Paige together with a hex, Dad would have a glamorous girlfriend instead of an ordinary one. A girlfriend who looks nice and classy all the time, who could teach me how to put on makeup and talk to boys someday when I care about that stuff. And then, when they got married, Sam and I would be sisters like we've wanted! Everything would be exactly like it should be. There's no doubt about it—we *have* to do this hex! But how? "So what would we do? To Terri, I mean?"

"I don't know," Sam says. "But she's taking up a lot of your dad's time. Time he could be spending with my mom."

"That's true," I say. "So should we hex her to stay away from my dad?"

"Why not?" Sam asks. "And we could make it really good for her. She could get a job that pays a lot more money. . . ."

"Or find a rich boyfriend with a big clean house, and no kid and no millipede!" I offer.

"Or she could move farther away—someplace awesome, like across town at the beach. Anything that would let your dad and my mom be together more."

"I say . . ." I stop for a dramatic pause. "We do it!"

"And the sooner we do it, the sooner we'll be sisters!" Sam says.

"Then let's do it soon!"

"Love it, love it, love it!" we both start shouting until Sam's mom looks over and tells us to quiet down. So we jump in the pool and do the rest of our shouting underwater.

* ✳ *

There's only one thing standing between me and Sam and our awesome plan to become sisters. It's long and red and on top of Terri's head.

I know *I'm* the one who's going to have to get a piece of her hair. I just don't know where or when or how.

But I have my opportunity that very night, when Terri comes over for Chinese food. She and Dad barely have a chance to talk because there's a lot I want to know. In between forkfuls of beef with broccoli, I ask Terri everything about her life that crosses my mind—all the things that could help while Sam and I concentrate on our hex.

"Terri, what do you do for a job?"

"Oh, I design graphics," she tells me. "Sort of like what your dad does for websites, but I do it for TV. You're artistic. It's something you might like doing someday. . . ."

"Do you make a lot of money? It doesn't look like you have a very big house."

"Cleo!" Dad says. "That's not polite."

"It's okay." Terri laughs. "I like my house, since it's only me and my cat. And I like living so close to you two."

"Dad doesn't have a lot of money, though," I tell her. "He has to pay for my school and we have to fix my teeth soon, and who knows what else?"

"Cleo!" Dad scolds again. "Have some more fried rice and leave Terri alone for a while."

I don't want to have to change my attitude, so I eat more Chinese food. But the whole time I'm looking and staring and gazing at Terri's long red hair and wondering how I could possibly get my hands on it. I can't get in a fight with her like I did with Madison; that would never work.

Then it hits me! I feel like I've been quiet for long enough, so I say it.

"Terri, how do you get your hair to be so straight and long with no tangles?" I ask. She and Dad look at me strangely because that had nothing to do with whatever they were talking about.

"Well, Cleo, it's called a *brush*," she says in a jokey voice. Which of course I knew, even though I don't like using one very often.

"But do you have a special *kind* of brush?" I ask, feeling like a brilliant detective on a TV show.

"When did you get so interested in hair care?" Dad asks.

"I guess since we've been spending so much time with Sam's mom."

"Oh, really?" Terri sounds surprised and looks at Dad.

"Yeah, her hair is so shiny and pretty and mine is always messy and knotty."

"Well," Terri says with a sigh, "how about we watch a movie after dinner and we'll attempt to brush your hair together?"

Ugh. I didn't want this task to end up causing *me* pain, but I guess when it comes to voodoo, you gotta do what you gotta do.

After dinner I follow Terri to our bathroom. I watch as

Terri picks up my brush and walks out, her long red hair swinging, like it's in slow motion. I don't follow yet; I'm just looking down at the floor, taking a breath, wondering if this is going to work.

And that's when a brilliant idea hits me—*blam!*—like that gigantic ball in crab soccer. The easiest answer is right in front of me on the bathroom floor. There's a little bit of dirt, some open magazines Dad reads when he's on the toilet, and . . . a few pieces of Terri's red hair! Making sure I hear Terri's footsteps far away down the hall, I bend down to the floor and carefully pick them up like I'm Albert Einstein studying matter.

I take two pieces of hair, tiptoe to my bedroom, and find my science notebook. Opening the plastic folder seems like the loudest noise in the world because I'm so afraid Dad or Terri will walk in and ask me what the *bleep* I'm doing.

Luckily Dad yells from the living room, so I know he's not nearby. "Cleo! What are you doing? Terri's here with a hairbrush waiting for you!"

"I'm checking on Millie. I'm coming!" I place the hairs in the plastic folder with Madison's leftover blond one, then slam my notebook closed and run to the living room. Dad has turned on a movie I know he and Terri will enjoy but that will make me want to sleep. There's no reason for Terri to brush my hair now, but I don't know how to get out of it.

So I sit on the floor in front of her while we watch TV, and I let her go crazy on my messy head. It always hurts when I try to brush my hair myself because I let the tangles and knots get out of control. But with Terri, it's not so bad. She holds my hair in a ponytail as she brushes the ends, so it doesn't hurt so much. Then on top she takes it slow and tries to be gentle. I say "ow" a couple of times—I can't help it—but in the end it feels kind of nice, especially when it's all done and she brushes it from top to bottom. Then she hands me the brush and I do it myself too. My hair has never felt so luxurious. I wonder if it's glowing like Madison's does.

"Well, that looks really nice," Dad says. "You should thank Terri for doing that."

"Thanks, Terri," I say, feeling guilty because I know what it was all for. I decide to go to bed and let them watch their movie together, because once Sam and I do the hex, there won't be nights like this anymore.

17

When I get to Kevin's classroom on Monday, Sam is already in her chair, sitting straight at attention and turned toward the door waiting for me. I can tell by her face that she's wondering about Terri's hair. As I walk by, I nod and whisper, "I got it."

She nods back with a wink. I don't think I've ever felt so proud.

At lunch we come up with the next part of the plan. Sam doesn't want to wait until the weekend, so she's going to ask her mom to invite us over for dinner during the week. "My mom and your dad can have a date, and we can do the hex."

"Okay," I say. "But your mom's gonna have to try really hard because my dad doesn't like me doing fun stuff during the week."

"Oh, I'll get it done," says Sam, and sure enough, she does. That night, I hear my dad on the phone saying, "I'm not sure, Paige. . . . We need our weeknights for home-work. . . . Cleo's not great at getting it done on time. . . ."

I interrupt, tapping on his shoulder. "What are you say-ing about homework? I can do it on time. What do you need? I'll do it early!"

"Hold on, Paige," he says, then turns to me. "If we go to dinner at Samantha's tomorrow night, I'd need you to prom-ise to get your homework done all week long."

"I promise, I promise!" I promise.

Dad looks at me for a second. I know he's not sure if he should believe me, so I give him my most honest and sin-cere face, with my eyes wide open and an adorable grin. He sighs and puts the phone back to his ear. "Okay, Paige, that sounds all right."

Yes! We're managing to get them together even *without* a hex! When Dad hangs up, I hug him and say, "Thank you, thank you! Sometimes you're the best dad in the world."

"Yeah, yeah, yeah," he says. "Tell me something I don't know."

"Ummm, female millipedes lay hundreds of eggs in a nest underground and they hatch after three months."

"Good one. I definitely did not know that. Now go do your homework."

"Do I have to?" I ask. But then I laugh so he knows I'm kidding, and I run to my room.

The next night, Dad looks like his usual self: baggy shorts, untucked T-shirt, and hair sticking up—and not in a cool, styled way like an LA actor. "Why didn't you dress up more?" I ask him in Sam's condo's elevator, wishing I had thought of it back home. I mean, the first time he brought Terri to our house, he cleaned it like she was going to be eating off the floor! Now when we're having dinner with his *next* girlfriend, his future *wife,* he can't even tuck in his shirt!

"Why would I?" he says. "We're just going to their house."

"At least pat your hair down," I whisper. "Sam's mom always looks so nice." And when Paige answers the door, she's dressed for a movie premiere or the ballet. As usual. Dad presses his hair down a little, but it doesn't help.

It's early for dinner, but Sam's mom leads us right into her dining room. The table is sparkling clean, with candles and even a bouquet of flowers in the middle. Like a real date, without us even trying! "I hope you don't mind, Bradley," she says, "but I ordered in from La Vibalatarenzifoo"—or some Italian-sounding name. "I'm not much of a cook!" She tosses her head back and laughs loudly. Dad doesn't.

"Where's Sam?" I ask. I don't like standing there near the adults with the voodoo doll in my backpack. I want to get down to business.

Sam's mom doesn't answer; instead she turns to Dad. "Bradley, I thought the girls might have more fun if they had pizza in Samantha's room while you and I enjoy an adult dinner."

"Sure," Dad says. At the same time I say, "Cool! Can I have a Coke too?"

Dad looks at me. I'm hoping he says yes since we're guests in someone's house. "Okay, one," he says. "But drink it soon, not later. I don't want you going to bed with high-fructose corn syrup coursing through your veins."

"Okay," I say, rolling my eyes a little. Paige whinnies her horsey laugh and hands me a Coke. Then I'm off running to Sam's bedroom.

"Sam, I know we're having pizza! And I bet it's the triangular kind!" I shout as I open her door. She looks up from her computer, where she's reading some kind of article. I look over her shoulder. The website she's looking at has pictures of ghosts and haunted houses, and phrases like "unexplained phenomena" and "paranormal mysteries."

"What's that?" I ask.

"It's a surprise. Do you want a surprise?"

"I always want a surprise," I tell her, "as long as it's a good one." I start to pull my backpack off my shoulders.

"Don't!" she shouts. "We're going out."

"What do you mean, 'out'?" I'm not happy with this surprise. I want dinner.

"I mean, like, not here."

"Then where?"

"I said it's going to be a surprise." I'm just staring at her, so Sam groans and then explains. "I was doing a little voo-doo research, and I read that sometimes people do spells in special places that help them communicate with the spirit world."

This sounds weird and scary, especially with Dad and Sam's mom right down the hall. I don't want to sound like a baby, though, so I just say, "What about the pizza?"

"We'll eat it later."

Ugh, I don't like this at all. I prefer my triangular pizza *hot*. "How about my Coke?" I ask. She doesn't understand a life where you can't have a Coke any time you want.

"Jeez, you can drink it later! What's the matter with you? I thought you liked action and adventure."

"I do!" I mean, I draw characters having adventures all the time. But Pandaroo and the Millipede with Many Shoes and even my villain Skunkifer don't have dads who can ground them and keep them from using the computer.

"I want a sister who likes to do the same kinds of things I do," Sam says, her hands on her hips. "If you're going to be a weeny wimp every time I want to do something fun, maybe we shouldn't be doing this at all."

Inside it feels like she grabbed a section of my heart and twisted it a little, but I say, "I'm not a weeny wimp!"

"Then come on," she says. "Do you have a jacket?" I silently show her the zip-up sweatshirt tied around my waist and she nods. "Good. It's getting dark out and it gets a little cold after dark."

"We're going *outside*?" I ask, realizing too late that this makes me sound both weeny *and* wimpy.

"Where else would we be going? To the *closet*?" She sounds a little snotty—like a certain person we know with the initials M.P.—but I'm not going to tell Sam that.

Sam has already opened the curtains and is pushing up one of her windows. I can see some purple sky above her building's rooftop, and I know it's going to be even darker soon. She already has one leg over the windowsill and is ducking out toward the outdoor hallway right outside the window. I'm glad we don't have to jump or climb down the side of the wall like in the movies, but I'm nervous.

I follow her anyway. What else can I do? Even with the way she just acted, she's my best friend, and if this hex works as well as the others, she'll be my sister. Sisters aren't always totally nice to each other and sisters fight sometimes. I'll have to get used to it.

I put one leg through the window, and it's easy to touch the ground on the other side. But when I try to push my way through, I can't. My backpack is stuck.

"Sam!" I shout.

She's halfway toward the exit sign at the end of the courtyard.

"Shhh!" she snarls. With a glare, she turns around and walks back toward me. "Do you want to get caught?"

"No!" I want to stay in her room, with pizza and Coke.

"Take off the backpack and hand it to me," she whispers.

I do, then climb through the window easily. She's already heading for a staircase.

So I chase after her, down the stairs and out onto the street. Though my legs are twice as long as Sam's, I can't keep up with her. She's carrying the backpack, but I'm the one starting to sweat.

We walk down a neighborhoody street with sidewalks and trees and houses, with apartment buildings in between. I can hear kids playing inside, smell food barbecuing in backyards, and see TVs glowing in windows. Then we reach a bigger street with lots of cars, Caffeine Craze (a coffeehouse I recognize because Dad likes it), a yoga studio, and a traffic light. Dad doesn't like me crossing streets like this by myself, and I can't really blame him, with my lack of focus and all.

None of this worries Sam, though. She pushes a button on the side of the traffic light and it makes a beeping noise. "Where are we going?" I ask. "This is kind of far."

"It's going to be totally worth it, don't worry," Sam promises. The light turns green and her feet are off the curb and flying across the street. I follow, imagining how Dad and Paige's cozy, delicious dinner could end at any time, and how they'll open Samantha's bedroom door to find neither of us inside. That would be big, big trouble.

Sam and I start walking by a fence that seems to go on forever. There's lots of grass and trees and bushes behind it, so at first I think it's a park. But when we come to the opening in the fence and turn down a small paved road, I see other things, like benches and flowers and different-shaped stones sticking out of the ground.

Gravestones.

"We're at a *cemetery?*" I don't know why I whisper because I'm not going to wake anybody up. "This is creepy!"

"No, it's cool. It's a place for us to communicate with spirits no longer of this world, like in the thing I was reading online," Samantha says, enjoying every moment of this. "Plus, this way I can take you to my favorite dead person."

"You have a favorite dead person?"

She's walking ahead of me, talking as she goes. "I don't *know* the dead person. But when my dad visits, we have picnics here and we always put our blanket on this guy. His gravestone is big and flat on the ground, and it's a perfect place to sit. It'll be a great place to do a hex!"

Okay, that's a little weird, but I guess I'll have to accept that when Sam and I become sisters, I'll have to picnic on dead people. At least when her dad's in town.

I follow Sam down paths and across grass and under a tree that has branches like long, bony octopus tentacles. Then she stops, takes off my backpack, and puts it down. "Here he is," she announces, standing in front of a large gray square in the ground. "Harold Rocap. 1910 to 1996. Eighty-six years old. Beloved husband and father."

I pull out my phone and turn on the flashlight to get

a closer look. There's a drawing of Harold on the shiny stone—sort of like a cartoon and sort of like a painting. He has a bushy mustache and old-fashioned glasses. At least he used to. Now those glasses might be the only thing left in that grave. Even his clothes would have disappeared into dust by now. Gruesome.

"So let's do it!" Sam says. I kneel down and open my backpack. But instead of thinking about the hex, I'm worried about getting dirt or grass stains on my knees. Dad might notice and wonder how they got there.

Sam's not worried about anything. "Come on!" she urges me.

"Okay, okay," I sigh. I pull out the voodoo doll, which is still wrapped in my drawing of Pandaroo. The paper has red stains on it from the wine we dipped the doll in. It kind of looks like blood, but that's the last thing I want to think about in a graveyard as it's getting dark outside. I unwrap the paper, realizing I haven't seen the doll since we put him away wet on the night of the last hex. I followed Uncle Arnie's recipe and kept him underneath my bed in the darkness.

The doll is dry now, but the tan material he's made of is stained red all over. It's sad seeing him messed up like this, with cinnamon grains stuck to him and oatmeal flakes falling off. There's a strange smell to him too—a little sour, a little like mud, but with the tiniest whiff of cinnamon. I hand him to Sam and take my notebook out of my backpack, holding my cell phone flashlight toward the plastic folder so I can see Terri's hairs inside. I pull out a strand with my finger and thumb and place it carefully on the doll's yarn hair.

"Okay, now remember, we have to concentrate as hard as last time. Even harder," Sam says.

Since we want Terri (and her entire body) to stay away from Dad, Sam puts the pin in the doll's middle. We sit down on top of the gravestone. I can feel the coldness on my butt even though I'm wearing jeans. I look down but don't want to close my eyes in this creepy graveyard. I don't believe in ghosts of dead people, but I never thought I believed in voodoo either, and look how that turned out. Best to keep my eyes open, stare at my wine-stained voodoo doll, and concentrate on Terri. I think about her brushing my hair . . . rolling pigs . . . sitting with Dad on the beach . . . but these aren't the right kind of thoughts, so I focus on her with a big sack of money from her new job making graphics for a huge TV station. She's moving out of her little house in our neighborhood and into a big mansion with a patio far away at the beach. I imagine her with her new rich boy-friend, and they're making dinner together, only it's in our kitchen and I'm there too. This is strange, and it feels like it's taking longer than usual. I can't help squirming a little.

I'm glad when the five minutes are over. Sam looks up, pleased. "Awesome, huh?"

"Yeah, that was fun," I lie, getting on my feet. A breeze blows across my sweaty arms and I shiver. The leaves make crinkling sounds above me and I look up. The trees look darker now, with their gnarly branches blacker than the purple sky. "We'd better go, though. We've got to walk back to your condo, climb through the window, and have dinner, and hope your mom and my dad aren't finished eating already."

"Stop worrying so much," Sam says. She takes her time putting the doll back in my backpack. "We have to give them time to keep falling in love. Plus, my mom says worrying gives you wrinkles and it's not a very attractive quality."

Paige would know things like that. She's going to be good to have around as I get older.

"I just don't want to get in trouble. Can we go?"

Sam zips the voodoo doll back up in my backpack and throws it over her shoulders. "Okay," she says. "Let's go." I can tell she's annoyed, but sometimes sisters act that way so I guess it's okay.

I wonder if there's always this much compromise involved with having a sister.

We walk back quickly. I can smell that the barbecues in the neighborhood are mostly over. I still see TVs in the windows, but I don't hear as many kids making noise inside. My heart is pounding when we go back through Samantha's bedroom window.

Sam must be hungry from all the walking too, because she sits right on the floor and opens the pizza box. We chow down finally, but it's not as delicious as I hoped it would be, not after all this time.

A little later there's a knock at Sam's door. Dad and Paige's date must be over.

"Hey, Cleo," Dad says. "Time to go."

Usually I'd beg to stay longer, but tonight I'm still jumpy from sneaking out and doing a hex in a graveyard, so I'm ready in no time. In the car on the way home, I hear my phone ding with a text. I'm expecting it to be from Sam, but it's not.

It says, Hey, it's Terri. Heard you went to Samantha's tonight. Hope you had as much fun as these two! Underneath there's a link to a cartoon that looks like she put it together herself. It's a super-cute monkey dancing with an even cuter millipede.

Since I've only ever gotten texts from Dad and Samantha, this is a really nice surprise. I didn't even know Terri had my phone number. Now when I think about her moving away or getting a new job or dating another guy, I feel a little bad.

But just a little.

18

I wake up in the middle of the night. It's completely dark out and my brain can only compute one thing: stink! Something smells, reeks, and is offensive to my nostrils! There's only one thing in the world that smells like this—at least only one thing I've ever smelled in my almost twelve years—*skunk*! One of those nasty black-and-whiters might as well have come into my bedroom, lifted its tail, and sprayed right up my nose; that's how close it smells.

Los Angeles is one of the biggest cities in the world, but sometimes in our neighborhood we see animals you wouldn't expect, like coyotes and possums . . . and skunks. It's not so bad if we're driving in the hills and we smell it far away, but when it's right in your bedroom, whew! Disgusting!

First there's the smell; then there's a yell. It's Dad. "Oh, no! Cleo, is Toby in your room?"

The smell just filled up my nose so I haven't had time

to look around. It's pretty dark, but I see Toby on the floor right next to my bed, his tongue hanging out, and I'm not kidding when I say it looks like he's *smiling*. Right away I figure out what must have happened. Toby went out through the dog door in the middle of the night and got himself into an argument with a skunk. Knowing Toby, he was probably just trying to make friends, but a skunk wouldn't understand that.

Dad opens my bedroom door. The hallway light is on, so I can see he's in a T-shirt and his underwear and his face is red like he swallowed hot sauce. "Toby!" he yells, putting a couple of curse words in there too. "Cleo, go take a shower and wash your hair as fast as you can; then go wait in the car so I can take you to school."

I look at my clock. It's 4:35 in the morning and school doesn't start until 8:30. I say this to Dad but I guess I shouldn't have, because he yells, "Would you rather sit in the house until then?"

I wouldn't rather do that, so I jump out of bed. Dad pulls Toby out of my bedroom by his collar. Toby's not smiling anymore. Now he looks ashamed.

In the shower, I almost feel like throwing up a couple times because the smell doesn't only fill my nose, it fills every part of my entire body, including my stomach. And I can't get rid of it, no matter how much soap and shampoo I use.

When I'm dressed and out of the bathroom, Dad goes

right in so he can wash off. I start to walk out of the house, but I hear Toby bumping around behind the closed door of the laundry room. Dad must have put him there so he doesn't get his smell all over more stuff. "Toby, are you okay?" I ask.

Whimper whimper whine.

"Did Dad put food and water in there for you?"

Whine whimper whine.

I don't want Toby to spend hours in the laundry room without anything to snack on, so I open the door a teeny bit to look inside. In the one second it takes me to spot his bowls, he pokes his nose through the crack of the door; then pushes through and jumps up on me.

"No, Toby! No, no, no!" I shout, pushing him back inside and closing the door. He definitely got a little more smell on me, but I zoom to the kitchen sink and wash my hands and arms with dish soap. Hopefully Dad won't notice.

I run down to the car and pretend like I've been there all along. Dad gets in a few minutes later. His hair is wet and he smells mostly like soap, but with a skunky aftersmell.

"Well, that was an adventure," he says. He actually doesn't sound so mad anymore. "So how about we go to the store to buy tomato juice and vinegar so I can clean Toby up later, and then we go to Wingberry's for breakfast?"

This sounds great! "Okay!" I say, and Dad pulls out of the garage.

At the grocery store, we push a cart down the aisles until we find what we need. When we unload the cans and jugs onto the counter, the lady knows our dog got skunked. "From what we're buying?" Dad asks.

"No, from the stench!" She laughs and we do too.

We get to Wingberry's, which is my favorite restaurant in all of California, at least since we moved here three months ago. It's a diner with fun pictures and cartoons all over the walls, and waiters and waitresses who always seem happy. Wingberry's has the biggest, most delicious juicy burgers and salty fries, and Dad once told me that it's open all day and all night long. But I've never been here at this hour. It's 5:52 a.m.

The waiter at Wingberry's knows we've been skunked too, but he thinks it's funny and asks what we want. Dad lets me have a burger even though it's breakfast time, and he orders cheesy eggs with onions and peppers. He also orders a ham, cheese, and egg croissant, and I figure that all the early morning excitement made him extra hungry. But before the food arrives, I see why he ordered so much. Of all the people in Los Angeles and the world, who walks past the front window and into the restaurant but Terri?

"What are you doing here?" I ask as she sits down next to Dad.

"Oh, I was just up at the crack of dawn and I got hungry and thought, Wingberry's is open, I'll go there."

"Really?" I ask.

Dad and Terri stare at me like I'm a skunk at a tea party. "What do you think?" Dad asks.

The answer is obvious but it seems too crazy to believe. What kind of lady comes out to breakfast at five in the morning with her boyfriend and his dumb kid? She must really, *really* like Dad. And after her text last night, I'm starting to think she likes me too.

"Wow," I say. "I wonder if Samantha's mom would ever do anything like this."

"Why?" Terri asks, with a glance at Dad. "What kind of stuff does Samantha's mom do?"

"Oh, she orders dinner from fancy restaurants, and has long red nails, and wears high heels, and tells Dad his cooking is scrumptious and stuff. She's got really pretty hair—I already told you about that—and all her clothes look like they're from Beverly Hills. And she's always wearing makeup, even at the pool." Then I realize that Terri doesn't even know Samantha's mom, so what does she care? In Focus! class, Roberta teaches us to consider how what we're saying affects other people, and to pay attention to whether they seem interested or not. So I change the subject back to Terri. "Why'd you come to breakfast?"

"Well, I don't have to be at work till nine, so maybe I'll go back to sleep afterward," Terri says. "After all, *my* house doesn't smell like skunk!"

"You're lucky," I tell her. "Because it stinks!"

"Actually," she says with a sniff, "I can smell it on you two a little."

"We know," Dad says, pretending to be ashamed like Toby. "But do you still like us?"

"You're buying me breakfast, so I like you fine!" Terri jokes, messing up Dad's wet hair with her hand. The food comes a few minutes later. I dig into my tasty burger as the sky gets lighter outside and it becomes morning for real. I'm having a pretty good time, but this is the opposite of what Sam and I concentrated on. In our hex, we wanted Terri to spend *less* time with Dad.

Did something go wrong? Or do we just have to wait a little longer?

At school, Samantha meets me at our classroom door. "So, did anything happen yet?" she asks.

"Not . . . exactly," I say, speaking slowly because lots of thoughts are suddenly coming into my brain.

"What does that mean? Has your dad heard anything from Terri?" Before I can answer, she keeps going. "No, wait, it's better if he *doesn't* hear from her. Do you know if he talked to her this morning?"

"Yeah, Dad's talked to Terri. We've even seen her."

"Before school? Why would you see Terri this early in the morning?" Samantha asks. "And why do you smell so weird? If you've started using deodorant, that is *not* the right brand. It smells like . . ."

"Skunk," I tell her. "Toby was skunked this morning. It woke me up at four-thirty. And Dad was mad at first, but then he invited Terri to breakfast and he felt better. But Dad *is* mad at Toby. He closed him in the laundry room so he can clean him up later."

"Did he jump on you after you got dressed?" Sam asks, picking something off my T-shirt. "You've got red hairs all over you." She holds a strand up to her nose. "Oh yeah, that's skunk!" she sneers, tossing it to the ground.

At that moment, I understand what went wrong. It all comes to me like a light turned on in the middle of the night. We concentrated on keeping Terri and Dad apart, but instead Dad got separated—this morning anyway—from someone else whose name begins with a *T*.

There's someone in our bathroom a lot more than Terri is. Someone with long red hair . . . who lies on the floor . . . and sheds.

The hair on the bathroom floor wasn't Terri's at all.

Now I just have to tell Sam.

I take a breath and work up the courage. "We used the wrong hair," I say.

"What do you mean 'the wrong hair'?" Then she looks down on the ground where she threw the hair she picked off my shirt.

Sam looks back at me. I can tell she understands.

Before I can say anything else, Lisa Lee and Kylie Mae push past us to get into the classroom. They obviously get a whiff of me, because they each make a face and Lisa says, "The piggy from Ohio smells like a skunk today!" With Madison gone, I guess she decided to take over her duties. Great.

"How did that happen? Toby's hair?" Sam asks.

"The bell's gonna ring," I say.

"So tell me fast."

Talking fast is my specialty, so I do it. "I didn't pick the hair off Terri's head, I picked it off the bathroom floor. It was long and red like Terri's so I thought it was hers, but it was Toby's. I didn't do it on purpose."

Sam looks at me and doesn't say anything. We both know I screwed up. Finally she says, "That sucks."

And before I can say anything back, the bell rings and we rush toward our seats.

"Well, you're going to have to get the right hair, and we're going to have to hang out after school again this week," Sam whispers as we sit. "I'll text my mom and tell her to work on it."

Kevin starts talking, so I can't discuss it with her anymore.

But I'm not listening to Kevin. I'm busy wondering how I'm going to get a piece of Terri's hair.

Her *real* hair.

19

Before Kevin even tells us to get out our homework, there's a knock at the classroom door. It's Andrea, the principal's secretary. She hands a note to Kevin, who reads it and then turns to me! "Cleo, your presence is requested in the principal's office."

"Why? What did I do?"

Kevin doesn't know. "Maybe it's an important message from home or something. Follow Andrea to the office, please."

Andrea walks way ahead of me, I bet to avoid my smell. When we get to Frederick's office, I stand in the doorway.

"Come in, Cleo," he says from behind his desk. I take a step inside. That's when I see three people sitting on some chairs to my right.

Madison, her dad, and her mom.

Now I'm worried. What am I doing here? Did they

figure out that I did hexes on her? Why just me and not Samantha too?

"Cleo, go ahead and sit down," Frederick tells me. "You know Madison," he says.

Duh, I think, but of course I don't say it. Madison and I nod at each other.

"Madison is coming back to school today, but I wanted her to talk to you first."

"And he wanted to have her parents here," Madison's dad says rudely. I don't know why he's mad at me. I didn't ask him to come.

"I've asked Madison to say a few words to you before she goes back to class," Frederick says.

Madison looks over at me and turns her chair a little. It makes a loud scraping sound that makes me jump.

"Ummm, well, Cleo . . . ," she starts slowly.

"Madison, I have a meeting at ten over in Santa Monica and traffic is brutal," her dad says. "Please don't draw this out."

Madison takes a breath and looks like she's thinking for a second. "I'm sorry, Cleo."

Wow. I don't know what to say. One word does fall out of my mouth, though. "Why?"

"I've been mean to you since you got to our school," Madison says.

"Unfair, not nice," Madison's mom whispers.

"I know, Mom," Madison whines; then she turns back to

look at me. "It was unfair and not nice. I had a lot of time to think while I was away from school, and I'm going to be nicer to you from now on. It's not your fault that you're new and you don't have the coolest clothes or friends. You can't help it."

Well, she *is* right about all those things.

"I'm not going to say bad things about you anymore. And I'm sorry."

She's sorry? This is crazy. I'm sorry for *her*! She farted up a storm in Focus! and then went crazy in science class, all because she said I had a clown's name and made a bunch of piggy jokes about me. She missed almost two weeks of school, and she had to stay home with her unpleasant and overtanned parents. And now, she's being nice. Maybe she's being forced to do it, but she's actually being nice.

It took a while—a week and a half, to be exact—but now I know for sure: the hex worked! So if I manage to really get a piece of Terri's hair this time, and Samantha and I concentrate and focus super seriously, we'll be able to get Terri away from Dad for real. Then we'll all be happy and we won't even have to do hexes anymore because life will finally be perfect. Everything can go back to the way it used to be before Terri—except for one extra-awesome addition: Sam will be my sister! I'm so full of positive juju that I want to jump out of my chair!

"So Madison is going to make the same apology in front of the class today," Frederick is telling me. I wasn't even paying attention, but I use one of Roberta's Focus! tips and try to fill in the blanks of what he was saying.

"You mean Madison is going to say the same kind of thing she just said to me? To the whole class?" I ask.

"Yes, that's what he just said," Mr. Paddington says in a jerky tone of voice.

"Oh, she doesn't have to do that." She's been through enough, having to stay home with that dad for more than a week. Plus, she's given me the best gifts of all time—more proof that voodoo works and the chance to have Samantha as my sister. Eventually.

"Cleo, are you sure?" asks Frederick. "We want to put this all behind us, once and for all. If that means Madison needs to apologize in front of the whole class, she will do it."

Madison looks at me with an expression I've never seen on her face before. Not snotty. Not scowling. She looks like she's making a wish. Like she's hopeful.

"I'm sure," I say. "I'm okay with her if she's okay with me."

Madison smiles—the first nice one I've ever seen. "I'm okay," she says.

Frederick stands up. "Then I suppose we're done here."

"Thank God!" Mr. Paddington says loudly as he gets out of his chair, which makes a louder noise than Madison's did. He walks out the door without even saying goodbye to Madison. Her mom follows but turns around.

"Bye, honey," she says, leaning down to give Madison

a kiss on the cheek. "You did that really well. I'll have Sonia make a special snack for you at home." As her clicking heels get quieter in the distance, I hear one more comment from her.

"What was that *smell*?"

Ha! I almost forgot about my skunking. Well, at least I made Heather and Henry Paddington sit in a room with me and suck it all in! I hope they take the stink home with them.

Frederick calls for Andrea to take me and Madison back to class. Madison and I walk next to each other but don't say anything. I go into the classroom first, and when Madison comes in after me, everyone gasps in surprise, even Lisa Lee and Kylie Mae. Didn't they know she was coming back today? They're her friends. If I had been out of school for over a week, you can bet Samantha would know when I was coming back.

"Welcome back, Madison," Kevin says. "Please take your seats. We're in the middle of the math homework from last night. The assignment was emailed to you."

I sit down. As Madison opens her backpack and pulls out her books, Sam gets my attention. I can tell she wants to know everything, but Kevin begins talking about fractions so she's going to have to wait. Inside, I laugh a little. It's kind of fun to know something she doesn't for once.

Over the next couple of days, Madison gets back into the school routine. I guess the only difference is that she doesn't call me a piggy or a clown. Sam thinks it's the coolest thing ever that Madison had to become nice and apologize to me, but she doesn't focus on that for long.

"You know what you're doing tonight?" she asks me Friday after school as we're waiting for our parents to pick us up.

"Dinner. Homework. Internet, I guess."

"Nope!" Sam says, excited. "My mom and I are following you and your dad home, and we're going on a hike and having dinner and then we're going to figure out a way to hex Terri. For real this time. I mean, now that Madison is back and nice, we know the doll is really, truly working. We'll be sisters . . . who knows how soon?"

"Maybe by summer!"

"We could go on vacation together!" Sam says.

Though our charms have put me in close contact with bad things, like smelly skunkings and parents like the Paddingtons, when I picture a trip to a Mexican beach or Disneyland or Africa, where African millipedes come from, I'm ready to do our next one. Our last one and our best one.

It's hard to believe that Dad agreed to me and Samantha hanging out again, but when he pulls into the parking lot he shouts through his open window, "Hey, Cleo, are you ready for a fun night?"

"Yeah!" I say, getting in the car.

"Sam, do you know the way to our house from here?" Dad asks.

"I sure do, Mr. Nelson," Samantha says with a super-sweet look on her face.

Sam and her mom get to our house a few minutes after we do. Paige walks in like a supermodel in her hot-pink zip-up hoodie and tight matching yoga pants. Dad asks me if I want to change into shorts before our hike, and before I answer, Sam interrupts. "Hey, Mr. Nelson? I was thinking on the way over here that maybe you and Mom could go on the hike by yourselves."

I look at Sam, my mouth wide open.

"Cleo and I have a lot of stuff to do for school, and I'm sure we'd be okay on our own if you were only gone for an hour or two."

Not only did Sam manage to create this date for Dad and Paige; she's getting us time to be on our own. She's so good at planning ahead. I need to focus on learning more from her.

"I don't know, Sam," Dad says. "I've never left Cleo alone like that."

"But she's not alone," Sam says. "We're together. We both have phones and you're not going very far, right?"

Dad looks at Paige, who says, "As young as Samantha is, she benefits from a strong independent streak that will make her a formidable young woman." I'm not sure what all that means, but I hope Paige lets me be independent and whatever formidable is when she's married to my dad! Paige keeps talking. "So maybe we take a short walk instead of a full hike . . ."

"And you can still go to dinner too!" Sam adds. "You can order food for me and Cleo."

Dad and Sam's mom talk it over for a minute, and though Dad doesn't seem very sure, he eventually says YES! He calls our favorite Thai food place and asks for delivery, and leaves me money to pay. Before he and Paige leave, they give us a million other instructions: if anyone comes to the door, look through the peephole before answering . . . call one of them if we have a question . . . call 911 if it's life or death . . . tip the Thai delivery guy five dollars . . . blah blah blah. It's all pretty boring and stuff we already know, but I can't help but be excited because Dad's letting me stay alone—well, almost alone. When Sam and I are sisters, this will happen all the time!

Finally they tell us to be good, and they leave. I watch as they walk down the path to the garage, Paige's butt swinging from side to side in her hot-pink yoga pants.

"Woo-hoo, they're gone!" Samantha shouts, running down the hallway toward my bedroom, her arms shooting out in all directions. If a spaz contest were being held right now, she might actually beat me. "And I have a great idea!" Her sneakers squeak as she slides to a stop by the bathroom door and runs inside.

I follow, but before I get there, Sam steps back out

holding a hairbrush. "Do you see what's in here?" she asks, pulling a clump of tangled hair out of the brush.

"Ewww," I say, but that doesn't stop Sam from pulling strands of hair out of the clump one by one.

"Black hair," she says, letting it fall to the ground. "Gray hair," she says next, dropping it. It's followed by a black hair, another black hair, another gray hair . . .

I watch as Samantha finds the one hair she's looking for and tosses the brush back onto the counter. I look closely at her hand. She's pulled a piece of long red hair out of the clump, and now it's hanging between her fingers. "I don't think *this* is Toby's," she says.

She's right again, of course. I wonder if I might get tired of that. Because I'm almost never right. "Let's get started," she says.

I'm ready. And after how wrong it went last time, I am determined to do this hex perfectly. Then the doorbell rings.

Toby barks and runs around in circles. "Ugh! Terri's fate postponed!" Samantha groans in a joking way as she pushes the red strand of hair into her jeans pocket.

"It must be the Thai food!" I say and run for the door, asking Sam to pull Toby into the bathroom and close the door so he won't jump on the delivery man. And that's who I expect when I peek through the peephole.

That's not who I see, though.

Who I see is Terri.

20

Terri is standing on our front step, holding a small pink cardboard box. It's the kind that usually comes from a bakery, but I'm so shocked and scared that I don't even care what kind of goodie she has.

I open the door. "What are you doing here?" I ask.

I must not say it in a very welcoming way, because she laughs and says, "Well, that's a fine way to greet someone who's stopping by to give you some cake!"

"Yum, cake!" says Sam, who is suddenly standing right next to me. "I love cake," she continues, sort of phony-sweet. "What kind is it?"

"It's birthday cake, left over from a party at my office." Terri hands me the box and turns to Sam. "You must be Samantha."

"Yep, you're a smart one!" says Sam, as cool and casual

as if she were talking to a kid at school, not an adult she's about to hex!

"Well, nice to meet you," Terri says. Samantha shakes her hand with the hand that was just going through the hair in Dad's brush. Gross.

"Nice to meet you too," Sam says. "Thanks for the cake, but we're busy, so we'll see you later."

Samantha starts closing the door, right where Terri is standing! Terri holds out her hand and says, "Cleo, is your dad here? I'd like to say hi before I go."

"No, he's out with my mom," Sam says.

I don't know much—anything, really—about boyfriend-girlfriend relationships, but I don't think Terri is supposed to know that Dad is basically on a date with Paige right now.

Then I realize why Sam is saying it.

"Yeah, they're going for a hike and then having dinner," I add. Like Sam, I'm trying to make Terri jealous too, though deep down I feel mean saying it. Being mean is the kind of thing Madison and her friends are supposed to be good at, not me.

"My mom said they might get a drink too, but I don't know if she meant coffee or wine or what," Sam says.

Terri's face changes. She's not her usual perky self. "Oh," she says. "I thought he said he was working on a project here at home tonight."

"No, he's out with my mom," Sam repeats happily. My face gets hot and I cough a little. This is definitely mean, and I've never been mean to anyone, not even a bug. It feels weird. And not comfortable at all. But inside I tell myself we're only doing this so Sam and I can be sisters, and then everything can be normal again. Even better than normal. Perfect!

"Okay," Terri says, her mouth so tight it barely opens. Then she takes a breath and says, "Well, Cleo, let him know I came by, and save a little cake for them." I nod, though I know Paige wouldn't eat it anyway. "Be careful here all alone, okay? You can always call me if there's an emergency."

"Okay, see ya!" says Sam, all cheerful. "But we'll call our parents if there's a problem."

Terri says goodbye and walks down the same path Dad and Paige walked down just a couple of minutes earlier. Her shoulders look slouchy and I feel a little sick to my stomach.

With Terri gone, Samantha is ready to put our plan into effect. "That was a close one!" she says, pretending to wipe sweat from her forehead. "Come on, let's do the hex!"

Sam runs down the hall. I follow more slowly. "Maybe we should wait until the food comes; I'm hungry," I say, though I'm really not.

When I get to my room, Sam is sitting at my desk, poking around on my computer. I'm really starting to be glad I don't have too much private stuff on there! "What are you looking for?" I ask.

"I think we should call your uncle Arnie before we do this one."

"Really?" I never pictured Samantha and Uncle Arnie talking to each other face to face. My dad calls Uncle Arnie "an acquired taste," meaning certain people don't get him right away . . . and I think Sam could be one of those people. "Why do you want to talk to Uncle Arnie?"

"Well, the last hex did not go well. . . ."

"But that's because we used the wrong hair!" I have a feeling Sam is blaming me, without saying it, for the last hex. She acts like I don't take it as seriously as she does, like it's not as important to me as it is to her. But it is! Anybody could have made that mistake with the hair! Anybody with a dog whose hair looks exactly like the hair of her dad's girlfriend who she wants to keep away by using a voodoo doll.

"It's time we got some professional input," Samantha says.

Though I have serious doubts that Uncle Arnie is a "professional" at anything, we decide to call him. Dad has set up my computer so I can dial him from my room now. After two rings, his screen comes on. If I wanted Sam to see him in his full weird glory, my wish has been granted. He must have just gotten out of the shower. He's wearing a light-blue robe with yellow duckies, and his hair makes him look like a wet cat. Like *his* cat, actually. "What's up, little niecey?" he asks, cleaning out his ear with his pinkie.

"Hey, Uncle Arnie, this is my friend Sam." Sam waves and Arnie waves back. "She and I were about to do another positive happy voodoo charm, but we wanted something extra special for this one. Like the time you sent me the recipe."

He thinks for a second, then snaps his fingers. "Okay, I know what you need." He starts to talk, but I have trouble listening because I notice that he doesn't have patches of hair on his chin or ears anymore, but there *is* a little bit growing out of his right nostril. With Uncle Arnie, it seems like hair doesn't go away; it just changes location.

When I pay attention again, he's in the middle of explaining something. "An incantation is a chant used for magic and sorcery," he tells us, "and when two friends use it together, the spell is certain to work better than ever before. After you put the pin into your doll, recite this five times, with more speed each time: *'As the thorn pierces the poppet, the juju opens the locket. You are free. So mote it be.'*" He pauses for a second, then grins like a goon. To my surprise, his teeth are gleaming white—no food particles in between! "I wrote it myself," he says. "Come on, say it with me!"

Sam joins right along immediately. It takes me a second, because (1) I don't even know what "mote" means, and (2) I'm thinking about how our first hexes worked fine without cemeteries and incantations. Well, sort of fine.

"Come on, say it!" Sam says. I feel uncomfortable but I do it anyway. What choice do I have? This hex has to work for Sam and me to be sisters. At first I mumble, but after a few times it gets kind of fun to say. We say it and say it until we're giggling, then laughing, then making mistakes because anything can become a tongue twister if you say it enough times in a row.

Uncle Arnie cheers us on from his sloppy living room in Louisiana. "I think you've got it!"

"Thanks, Uncle Arnie," I say. "We're gonna go now and try it out."

"All right, be careful, you two." Uncle Arnie lifts his cat up to the camera. "I've got to give Fuzzer a bath, and it's a perfect time. My tongue is perfectly clean right now!" He pretends to lick the cat and the screen goes black.

"So, that's your uncle," Sam says uncertainly. "He's pretty weird."

Well, she's not wrong, but he *is* my uncle, and I like him. And now that I think of it, once Sam and I are sisters, he'll be her uncle too. So she'll have to accept him no matter how strange he is. I hope she can.

"Okay, time to get serious," Sam says. So I do. I slide under my bed and take the doll out of his box. We sit on the floor, cross-legged as usual. Sam pulls Terri's strand of hair from her pocket and winds it around a piece of the doll's yarn hair. Then she pulls the pin out, holds it up, and asks, "Do you want to do it?"

"Ummm . . . okay," I say, slowly taking the pin from

her. For a second I sit there, still remembering Terri's face when she heard about Dad being out with Sam's mom.

"Well, come on, do it!" Sam urges.

Deep down I don't want to, but when I look into Samantha's eager eyes, I know I don't have any other choice. Since I don't want Terri and Dad to see each other anymore, I decide to push the pin into the doll's face. Then I pull my fingers away, happy to be done with it. All that's left is for Sam and me to say the incantation together.

"As the thorn pierces the poppet, the juju opens the locket. You are free. So mote it be."

As we say it, I concentrate on Terri walking to her car just now. That's good—in my imagination, she's walking away. She and Dad are apart. She's wearing regular jeans and a T-shirt, not tight yoga pants and lots of makeup. Her red hair looks nice, but not perfect like Paige's.

"As the thorn pierces the poppet, the juju opens the locket. You are free. So mote it be."

I think about Terri and Dad laughing together on the beach and how Dad never laughs at the stuff Sam's mom says. I know my brain shouldn't be going down this path, but I can't help it. Dad doesn't laugh with Paige. He doesn't want to have a drink with her or stay at her house when we hang out together. They only went on a hike and had dinners together because Sam and I forced them to, not because Dad wanted to. Dad likes Terri. Terri likes Dad. And now that I've seen Terri walking away from our house tonight, I feel bad for messing with that.

"*As the thorn pierces the poppet, the juju opens the locket. You are free. So mote it be.*"

I definitely want to be sisters with Sam, and live in the same house, and maybe share a room and spend all our nights and weekends and free time together, but is this the only way it can happen? Maybe Sam's mom and my dad should get together if they *want* to, not because we make them.

"*As the thorn pierces the poppet, the juju opens the locket. You are free. So mote it be.*"

But even if it's not what Dad wants, *I* want him and Paige to be together. I want me and Sam to be sisters. So I hurry and imagine Terri in her car, driving to a big house far away, with a new boyfriend and a great job, but I can't concentrate because it's the fifth time I'm saying the thing about the poppet and the locket and I know my time is running out. . . .

"*As the thorn pierces the poppet, the juju opens the locket. You are free. So mote it be.*"

And then the incantation is over. Sam locks eyes with me and I force a smile. I'm relieved I don't have to think about anything anymore—just fun. The Thai food arrives and Sam and I stuff our faces with noodles and shrimp and chicken and rice. Afterward, we eat two pieces of the cake Terri dropped off, and we play a game of Pig Mania. I feel guilty eating Terri's cake and playing Terri's game with Sam, but we still have a pretty fun time.

An hour or so later, Dad and Paige come back. I tell Dad that Terri came over and brought cake and there are two pieces left. Dad looks surprised for a second, then says to Paige, "Would you like a piece of cake?"

Like I predicted, Sam's mom says no. "After that meal we had, Bradley, I may never eat again," she says, holding her hands over her stomach.

"Oh, you barely ate anything," he says back, and she giggles. He doesn't laugh.

"Well, thanks, but I doubt the girls did any homework while we were gone, so we'd better go home and start on it."

Sam doesn't complain like I would; she just says okay and runs back to my room. She's ahead of me and by the time I join her, I see something I don't like at all.

Sam has the voodoo doll in her hand.

"What are you doing?" I ask.

"I want to keep it with me for a while," she says. "For safekeeping."

"What do you mean?" I ask. "It's safe here."

"Look, if we're going to be sisters, we're going to have to share things, so I should get to keep the doll this time." I have a hard time arguing with that, but still, it's my doll, not hers.

"What if your mom sees it?"

"I'll hide it. I've got a great place in the back of my closet under all the old baby dolls and toys I don't play with anymore."

"But why? Why do you want it?"

"I just do. Are you going to share or not?"

I don't know what else to do, so I just say, "I guess so."

The doll disappears into her open backpack. And though I haven't liked the feeling of having the doll in my room ever since I saw Madison and her parents together, I also don't like the feeling of it being somewhere else.

21

The next week at school, something new is happening. There's going to be a play. Our Focus! teacher, Roberta, wrote it, and it's called *Healthyland*—about a girl who goes to sleep one night and wakes up in a magical land full of people who love health and nutrition and movement and art and music. It sounds weird but fun. Roberta tells us that everyone in school can audition for the play, but she's hoping Focus! students will participate, because it would be a great learning experience for us and an opportunity to meet new people and make new friends.

"Ugh!" Samantha whispers to me. "Why would I want to be friends with any of these kids?" I don't really know what she means by that, since we were both happy for the five hours we were popular. "You and I have each other, and we don't need anybody else!"

I agree with her, but I don't think that's a reason not

to try out for the play. I'm actually excited about the idea. Being in a play would be fun. I mean, I'm probably not pretty enough to be an actress in real life, and I might talk too fast for people to understand me, but I know I'm loud enough for sure!

Roberta says we're allowed to skip our last class on Thursday to come try out, and whoever wants to audition can get a description of the play and a list of the characters from her. Lots of people raise their hands, including Scabby Larry, but I don't want Samantha to know I'm interested, so I keep my hand down. But when we walk out of class, I sneak over to Roberta and quietly ask if I can have some pages.

"Of course you can, Cleo! I was hoping you'd raise your hand. You're pretty quiet in class, but I have a feeling there's a big personality under there that would be great onstage."

"Really?" I ask. I don't think anyone has ever said something like that to me before.

"Yes, but I can't make any promises. Read this information before the audition, and if you make it through that one, you'll have to memorize a few things and try out a second time. That's called a callback."

"Cool, I hope I get a callback," I say, feeling very theatrical already.

I can't keep my secret from Samantha for long. At lunch she's in line getting macaroni and cheese while I sit at our table opening a sandwich called a panini that Dad bought at a Cuban café. Across the room I see Madison at her usual table with Kylie Mae and Lisa Lee, but things look different. Lisa Lee is the one gabbing and gesturing, flashing a big fake smile, and talking to boys, while Madison quietly looks out the window. For a second I think I know how she feels. Before Samantha and I became friends, I always felt alone at lunchtime, even when there were people all around me.

"What are you reading?" Sam suddenly asks, dropping her tray on the table. Her big square mound of bright-yellow mac and cheese wiggles but doesn't fall apart.

I'm caught. I can't come up with a lie, so I have to tell her the truth—sort of. "Well, I'm not sure, but I thought, just *thought,* that *maybe* I would try out for the play."

"What?" Samantha shouts, and I'm afraid a piece of the mac and cheese might fly out of her mouth and hit me in the face. "It sounds so stupid!"

"I probably won't get a part anyway," I say. "But it's not a bad way to get out of forty-five minutes of social studies."

"So you want to be an actress now? Like Madison Paddington?"

Even though Madison apologized to me, I don't want to be compared to her. "No, I just think it'll be fun to try."

Samantha leans back and takes this all in. "Okay," she says, but I can tell it's *not* okay. "If you need to do something like that, then good for you. Even if it's without me. Go ahead and meet new people and make new friends, and don't worry about me at all."

"You can try out too, Sam. I want you to!"

"No, it's fine." She takes a few more bites of her mac and cheese. I poke through my panini to see if there's anything in it I won't like, but it's just ham and cheese flattened on toast. It's weird for things to be so quiet between us.

Finally Sam says, "Hey!" and I jump back a little. "I wonder if anything's happened to Terri yet. When do you see her next?"

"I'm not sure," I say, chewing.

"You'd better text me the second something happens. And remember every minute of these auditions you're going to. I want to hear how dumb everybody looks."

I tell her I will, and I keep eating my panini.

When it's time for the audition on Thursday, I'm surprised by one person leaving Kevin's class. Of course Scabby Larry gets up, but so does Madison! I never thought a semi-professional actress like her would want to be in a school play with a title like *Healthyland*.

Scabby Larry walks next to me on the way to the Focus! room. "Isn't Samantha trying out?" he asks.

"No," I say, walking ahead in case Sam sees us.

"That's too bad." He's clearly not noticing that I'm trying to keep our conversation short. "We were in a play together in second grade and we had a great time."

Wow. Sam never told me anything about that! "You did?"

"Yeah, it was a lot of fun and we were, like, good

friends. I don't know what happened after that, but she was really great in the play. We were pilgrims, and she was my wife and said something about crushing cranberries for Thanksgiving."

Maybe that's why Samantha didn't want to try out. She wouldn't want to be Scabby Larry's wife again!

When we get to the Focus! room, Roberta has pushed all the tables and chairs to the side so there's a big empty space on the floor. There are pillows, instruments like a tambourine and a xylophone, and old-fashioned toys like a wooden train and a stuffed animal horse head on a stick. Healthyland looks like an even weirder place than I thought.

Roberta tells us to sit on the floor. I look around at all the other people. They're just kids in school like me, but for some reason I'm getting nervous. Right then, Roberta says no one should be worried, that this will be a "nontraditional" audition, which means there will be a lot of play and silliness and that everyone should just have fun.

First Roberta puts on music and tells us to "let loose," meaning we can kick, dance, do jumping jacks, or whatever we want. No one does anything too wild at first, but then Scabby Larry does a cartwheel! He's really good at it, but I'd be scared to do something like that in case I messed up and fell over and everyone talked about it forever. But in a few minutes everyone is laughing and whooping, and no one seems so worried anymore. So I do a goofy dance move my dad does that makes him look like a chicken who had too much high-fructose corn syrup, and I'm not embarrassed at all.

After that we do "vocal exercises," which for Roberta means opening your mouth really wide, making strange noises, and not being afraid to look stupid, which everyone does—including Madison, who doesn't seem to mind how she looks. But I decide right then that I'm not going to tell Samantha too much about this. Everybody looks equally dopey and it wouldn't be fair to single someone out for Sam's enjoyment. Even sisters don't have to share everything.

After our bodies and mouths and vocal cords are "loose," Roberta says people will pair up and do scenes, but not with lines written on a page. It's called improvisation, which is a fancy way of saying that you make things up as you go. I can't believe it when the first two people Roberta calls are me and Madison.

We both stand up, taking our time. As we walk toward the middle of the room, I realize that we've never had a real conversation. Even when she gave me her forced apology, I never actually spoke directly to her. This is a very odd way to begin.

"Let's pick a place where these two characters could be," Roberta says to everyone else. A girl I don't know yells out, "A farm!" Uh-oh. This could be bad. Piggies live on farms.

Madison and I look at each other, not sure what to do. Roberta says one of us should pretend to be a character that might be on a farm and start talking. So I do. "Howdy, pardner," I say in a Southern sort of voice, though I sound more like a cowboy than a farmer. "Welcome to Rassafrassa Farm!"

Madison gets down on her hands and knees. I wonder what she's doing . . . and then she *moos*! "Howdy, farmer," she says back. "I ran away from my last farm and I'm looking for a place to stay. Mooooo!"

I look at Roberta and the other people in the room, but they're just watching. So I look back at Madison on the floor and say, "Oh my garsh! A talking cow! I bet I can make money with you!"

Roberta and the kids laugh—in a good way. So Madison and I keep talking like a farmer and a cow, making a business plan to entertain the people of Ohio (I added that!), and people laugh the whole time—especially when I tell the cow to follow me back to my farmhouse, and I grab the horse head on the stick and pretend to ride off on it, with Madison following and mooing.

Other kids do improvisation scenes too. Some are funny and some are dumb, but it doesn't really matter because we're all having a fun time, and Roberta was right: it doesn't feel like the scary auditions I've seen on TV.

When we're finishing up, Roberta says everyone is invited to come to callbacks, which will be held next Monday after school. She hands us all a few pages from the script and tells us to read them and decide on the parts we might like to play. As I get up, I realize I don't even care if I get to be in the play or not, because that was a new and interesting experience.

"See you at callbacks!" Scabby Larry shouts as he runs to get picked up from school. "Actually, I'll see you tomorrow first!"

I wave, just a little, and take my time walking across the courtyard. I don't realize until a minute later that Madison is right next to me. I look at her for a second, and I think she looks at me, but we don't say anything until we're almost at the parking lot.

"How did you feel about the audition?" she asks. Outside of our goofy little scene, it's the first time Madison Paddington has ever spoken to me like a real person.

"It was cool," I say, then wonder if "cool" is a cool word to use around her.

"I thought so too," she says. "You were good."

I almost stop walking, I'm so shocked. She gets a step or two ahead of me. "Thanks," I finally say. "You were too."

I'm not sure, but Madison and I may have just had a friendly conversation. Our first ever.

It makes me wonder if there will be another one.

22

That night, instead of memorizing the countries of the world on the map, which we're going to have a test on, I'm in my room with Millie and Toby, reading the pages from the play script. I decide I don't want the role of the little girl who hits her head and ends up in Healthyland. She'll have too many lines and too much memorization, and I don't want the pressure. I want to be one of the people she meets along the way. "Would you like some kale? You can add it to your smoothie!" I say out loud, as if I'm the character called Healthy Eater. I try to make it sound somewhat realistic and even watch myself in the mirror as I say it.

I hear Dad's phone ring down the hall. It's not a real ring; it's an old song that Dad sings in a funny low voice when he's acting silly. *"It's not unusual to be loved by anyone."*

It's Terri's ringtone, but it doesn't sound like he's talking to Terri. "Yes, this is he," he says, all formal and serious. He never says *"This is he."*

I creep to my doorway so I can hear better. "Where is she? Is she okay?" When I hear that, my stomach suddenly twists and churns and flops upside down like a fish with a hook in its mouth, and my heart gets a cramp in it, like my leg sometimes gets in Recreational Wellness.

"I'll be right there," Dad says, and clicks off the phone. "Cleo!" he yells. "Put on your shoes!"

I know I should just do it but I still ask why, shouting down the hallway.

"We've got to go!" I can hear him moving around, maybe putting on his shoes, definitely grabbing his car keys. "I'm leaving," he says. "Are you coming or not?"

I'm not sure I want to go wherever he's going, but the idea of staying home and wondering is worse, so I grab my sneakers and run down the hall. He's already at the front door and doesn't even notice that my shoes are in my hands.

"What happened?" I ask, following him down our front path, trying to skip lightly so I don't hurt my feet on anything.

"Terri was in a car accident."

My heart gets even tighter and I could almost throw up, but I know I'd better not because Dad is in a hurry because his girlfriend was in a car accident and it's all my fault. This isn't what we wished for. Sam and I only wanted Terri to be apart from Dad; we didn't want anything bad to happen to her! But after everything that's happened with all the other hexes, I probably should have known better.

As I'm putting on my shoes in the car, I ask Dad what happened. He says "I don't know" in a real nervous, short way, so I don't ask him more. I look out the window and try not to cry. If he saw me crying, would he know this was my fault? Or would he just think I was sad, like when Marty died?

I watch the scenery pass by for a long time: a sign for a garage sale, a building with Mexican-sounding music coming out of it, little houses with paint peeling off, a store with Asian characters on it. I don't know which country they're from because I haven't memorized all the Asian countries yet, and there are a lot of them, and . . .

"Please stop singing," Dad says, a little harshly.

I had no idea. I guess when I heard the Mexican-sounding music, I started singing a song we learned in Spanish. It's about a mother hen who has to feed her babies, and it has all kinds of words we'll never need to use in real life, like *chicks* and *wheat* and . . .

"Oh my God," Dad says as he stops the car. I turn—and I see what he sees.

Terri's maroon car is on the other side of the road, and it looks like another car made a big metal fist and punched it in the side. *It's not my fault; it's a coincidence,* I say to myself. I don't believe it, but I'm thinking it so hard, I'm afraid I may say it out loud. Now I remember that I even thought of

Terri *driving*—driving to her new house with her new boy-friend and new job. No matter how much I say the opposite in my head, this *is* my fault.

There's a police car with its lights flashing and a big fire truck, even though nothing's on fire. The super-loud whoop of a siren suddenly hurts my ears. I turn around and see an ambulance pulling up. I don't know if that's a good thing or a bad thing. Does Terri need to go to the hospital because she's hurt . . . or because she's dead?

Don't be dead, I think. It might've even come out of my mouth, but Dad doesn't hear it because he's getting out of the car and yelling at me to stay where I am.

He rushes over and talks to a police officer, who points down the sidewalk. I follow his hand and notice Terri the same time Dad does. She's not dead! She's sitting on the curb and staring at nothing, with a scarflike thing tied around her neck, holding her arm against her middle.

Dad sits down with Terri and tries to hug her, but he can't because of her arm. So he gives her a kiss on the cheek and pushes her hair out of her eyes.

I keep watching as Dad takes Terri by her other arm and helps her step into the back of the ambulance. He stands behind her, making sure she gets in okay (I bet he says "fin-gers and toes, fingers and toes"), and he doesn't turn away until the doors are closed.

He should walk back to our car now, but he doesn't. He stands there for a minute, his head and shoulders down.

I start quietly singing the Spanish song about the mother hen, and I'm halfway through it before Dad finally turns and walks back to me.

He gets in the driver's seat and I ask how Terri is. He answers slowly. "She's fine. She's going to be fine. They think she broke her wrist and her nose. And she might have a concussion."

"What's that?"

He's still talking slow. "It's, um, if a person hits her head, her brain gets scrambled a little."

"What?" I ask. If Terri's brain is scrambled, I would never, ever forgive myself. I was the one who put the pin in the doll's head!

"It's not too serious," Dad says. "It usually goes away pretty quickly with rest." He starts the car. I stay quiet for once in my life, and it pays off, because Dad finally tells me what's happening. The ambulance is taking Terri to the hospital, and after the doctors take a look at her, we can say hello.

I've never been in a hospital before. It's not like it is on TV. It's not so clean and sparkly, and there aren't a bunch of beautiful people running around yelling "Stat!" The long thin lights on the ceiling make the place shadowy, and the people in their blue tops and pajama pants, even though they're doctors and nurses and stuff, look sickly as they shuffle down the ugly hallways. It feels like the real hospital shut down and was taken over by zombies.

A lady—a nurse, I guess—is leading us to the room that Terri's in. The lady's white sneakers make squishy sounds against the floor, and it's really annoying. I almost want to ask her if she can take them off and walk in her socks, but I'm sure she can't do that with all the needles and whatever germs are probably crawling around.

I can't hear everything the nurse and Dad are saying because they're too far in front of me, but I hear words like "bone" and "fracture" and "recuperation." Then we walk into a big room. There's a lot of whispering, a couple of coughs in the distance, and a buzzing from the lights that's even more annoying than the nurse's squishy shoes.

Terri is in a bed inside a little "room" made from pink curtains that hang from the ceiling. Instead of her usual pink cheeks and perky smile, she has bandages across her nose and black bruises under her eyes. She's got a cast on one arm, so she lifts the other one to wave a halfhearted hello.

"How are you?" Dad asks, giving her a kiss on the cheek.

"It could've been worse." She seems sad, but I guess that makes sense.

"What happened?" he asks.

Terri talks slower than she normally does. "I was driving down Fountain, and a car that was making a turn hit the side of my car, hard. My wrist," she says, lifting the cast off the bed a few inches, "hit the door on my side. And I don't know how I broke my nose. Maybe my face hit the steering wheel or something."

I can tell Dad doesn't like hearing any of that. I don't either. Especially when I remember pushing the pin into the voodoo doll's face, even though deep down I didn't want to.

"Did it hurt when it happened?" I ask.

"No," she says. "I guess I was in shock. That means you don't feel the pain even though it's there."

"Shock is good then," I say.

"I guess so."

We all sit quietly for a second, looking at each other with nothing to say.

This is bad. Really bad. This is much worse than farting or cursing or even being suspended from school for two weeks. It would have been fine if Terri just went away somewhere, but no matter how much we want Samantha's mom and my dad to get together, we didn't want Terri to get hurt. At least I didn't. I feel worse than I did when Marty died, even worse than when I realized I didn't have a mom. I never knew my mom, and nothing I did ever hurt her. So this may be the worst I've ever felt in my life.

I have to text Samantha, or call her, or even see her somehow tonight and tell her that this is over. We can't do any more hexes, no matter how great we think they'll be for us.

"They told me you can leave soon," Dad says. "Do you want to stay with us? That way Cleo and I can help you. Make you food, help you get changed . . ."

"Brush your hair!" I chime in, way too loud and happy for an ugly zombie hospital.

"Thanks, Cleo," Terri says with a small smile. "But my parents live forty-five minutes away. I'm going to stay with them for a day or two."

So that part of the hex worked too. She's moving farther away—at least for a while.

"Hey, Cleo, could I talk to your dad alone for a little bit?" Terri asks.

Dad says sure without asking me, but I don't complain. "I hope you feel better," I say as I leave the pink-curtained room, but I don't go far; I just sit on a plastic chair by a sink right outside. I can hear pretty much everything they're saying. Terri says she doesn't need Dad's help; her parents will come to the hospital to pick her up. She says Dad's been "preoccupied" for a while now—with work and me and my friends and my friends' *mothers*—so maybe it's time for them to have a little space from each other.

I start a video game on my phone and turn up the volume. I don't want to hear anything else. And sound effects on a game are a lot more fun to hear than people coughing and barfing, and lights buzzing and sneakers squishing, and Terri telling Dad that she doesn't want to be his girlfriend anymore.

Back home, Dad is as quiet as I am. He asks if I want to watch TV with him, but I say no, I'd rather go to bed. Dad is surprised, but he lets me go, saying it's been a long day for both of us. I think it's going to be a longer day— and night—for Terri. I wonder if she's still at the hospital, waiting for her parents. I wonder if her shock has worn off and if her nose and wrist are hurting her. Most of all, I start to wonder if she and I were ever friends. Or if someday we could *be* friends. Is that even possible?

Before I turn off my light, I pick up my phone and send Samantha a text.

No more hexes.

23

In the morning I don't want to get out of bed. It's just like the times before the voodoo doll, when I didn't like going to school and Dad would have to yell two or three times before I'd get up.

When he finally says, "I'm not kidding, Cleo; I am not in the mood for this," I roll onto the floor. My foot lands on my phone, which I tossed on the ground after texting Samantha last night. When I pick it up, I see that she wrote back. All her text says is: **What?!** ☹

I can tell from the frowny face that her text is extra serious. We'll have to talk about it at school.

I'm waiting for Sam in the courtyard before class when Scabby Larry walks up to me. "Hey, are you excited about callbacks?" he asks. "You were really good at the audition."

While I appreciate the compliment, I can't enjoy it. I

have bigger things on my mind right now. "Thanks. You too," I mumble.

"Have you thought about what part you might want?"

I don't want to be rude when he's being so friendly, but I see Sam coming in from the parking lot. Her head is down low and when I try to get her attention, she walks straight by. I know she saw us!

I excuse myself from Scabby Larry and rush to Kevin's classroom. Sam is already sitting, looking down at her desk like there's something really interesting there. The bell rings and I have to sit too, but I still whisper, "Sam!"

Finally she looks at me. She's got the same frown as the emoji in her text.

During history class, Kevin shows a movie about World War I. It looks boring, but there's too much going on in my brain to snooze. I expect to feel a note from Sam poking in my butt cheek, but nothing comes.

When the bell rings for lunch, Samantha leaves without me. She's obviously avoiding me, but I'll be able to corner her in the cafeteria. I go to the bathroom first and get my phone out of my backpack. I know this is a bad idea because I could drop my phone into the toilet, which is about the grossest thing I can think of, and it's a miracle it hasn't happened to me yet. So I'm ultra careful. I look at my messages and there's a ton of texts.

What are you talking about?! ☹

This is the best time we've ever had! ☹

I thought we were friends! ☹

Don't you want to be my sister? ☹

I don't know when Samantha had time to send all of those, but she must have been very sneaky because it's easy for a teacher to see the glow of a phone, especially during a movie. The same frowny face is on every text, but I feel like those faces are getting madder and madder at me.

In the lunchroom it's pizza day, which reminds me of how this whole thing got started, how great it was, and how happy we were to learn voodoo was real. I don't feel like that now. I wish I'd never gotten the doll. I wish I'd listened to my dad. I wish Sam and I had never started this.

I'm already sitting at our usual table when I see Sam walk across the cafeteria with her tray. I'm hoping that once Sam gets some food in her belly, she'll be ready to talk like normal friends.

She sits across from me but doesn't say anything. I open my recyclable lunch bag, and the Velcro makes the loudest, scratchiest sound I've ever heard.

I'm not sure what to say, so I just smile. It doesn't work because she's looking down, sopping up the pepperoni grease pools with a napkin, so my smile only reaches her mop of hair.

I open my sandwich. Dad used too much wax paper so it takes forever to open, and it's the loudest wax paper I ever heard. It *scrape scrape scrape*s with every fold I undo.

As I take a bite of my sandwich, I notice Sam's eating

her pizza. I feel like I'd better say something, so with my mouth full I ask, "How's the pizza?"

"How do you think the pizza is?" she asks, weirdly loud—much louder than my scratchy lunch bag or endless wax paper.

"Um, I don't know. Is it good this week?"

This time she talks even louder. "I don't know, Cleo, why would the pizza be any different this week than any other week?"

This is not good.

"WHY ARE YOU EVEN SITTING HERE, CLEO?" Sam says, yelling now. I start to see other people paying attention. Scabby Larry looks up from his phone and Kylie Mae pokes Lisa Lee and points toward me. "DON'T YOU WANT TO HANG OUT WITH ALL YOUR OTHER FRIENDS? ALL YOUR NEW AND BETTER FRIENDS FROM THE PLAY?"

I look around the room. It seems like the lunch ladies aren't even making noise anymore. I don't hear one piece of silverware clinking. I don't hear one dish being put on a tray.

I want to tell Sam that *she's* my best friend, and trying out for a play and not wanting to do hexes anymore doesn't change that. But before I can even open my mouth, she's shouting some more.

"NO ONE WANTED TO BE YOUR FRIEND WHEN YOU GOT HERE, AND NOW I KNOW WHY! YOU *ARE* A PIGGY FROM OHIO. YOU ARE A

SELFISH PIGGY WHO ALWAYS WANTS MORE FUN
AND MORE FRIENDS AND MORE FOOD!"

She picks a pepperoni off her pizza and throws it at me.
It stings, but not because it's hot.

"Let me tell you what happened," I say.

"I know what happened," she says back, throwing
another pepperoni that I wave away to the floor. "Your dad
told my mom. Terri hurt her nose and wrist. And now you
want to stop? She hurt her nose and wrist so you don't want
to be my *sister* anymore?"

"That's not it," I say, but she's not listening.

"No, it's okay," she says, though her angry voice tells
me it's not. "I thought you wanted to be sisters but I guess
you're *fine* with your fun dad and your cool dog and audi-
tioning for plays with Scabby Larry and Maddy Paddy. And
I don't have anyone!"

"You have *me,* Sam! I'm still your friend!"

"Friends can leave. Sisters stay forever!" she yells. Then
she throws one more pepperoni at me and picks up her tray.
"I'd throw the whole pizza at you but I like it too much!"
She stomps out of the lunchroom. I don't know where she's
going but I can't make myself get up and follow. I'm in
shock. Like Terri was. In my head I know this is painful,
but I don't quite feel it.

I stare down at the table at my PB&J, but I'm not hungry. Then I look at my shirt. There are three greasy little
pepperoni stains on it. I don't even care.

I start hearing sounds again. Forks and knives start clinking. People start talking. I'm sure they're talking about me and Samantha, but there's nothing I can do about it. I think about Jane Anne in Ohio, who decided she was too cool for me and stopped being my friend. That was hard, but at least she didn't do it like this—loudly, and in front of the whole school.

"Are you okay?" a voice asks me. I look up from my T-shirt.

It's Madison.

I can't really form an answer; all I can do is squeak out a noise that's not a word.

"I just wanted to make sure you're okay," Madison says.

This is a surprise, and it might be a nice one too, but I'm too much in shock to know for sure.

It's a sad, sad weekend. The saddest I can ever remember. Dad has lost his girlfriend, and I've lost Sam, my only real friend ever. I don't have anyone to hang out with besides Toby and Millie, and they don't talk and tell jokes and laugh about the people in school. But in a way I guess they're better, because they don't make me do things I don't want to do. Toby and Millie let me be myself.

I can tell Dad is sad too. He doesn't open the curtains, but I know it's a typical sunny Los Angeles weekend by the sliver of light that sneaks in the corner of the window.

Usually on a day like this, Dad will say something dorky like, "It's a magical day in California!" and suggest we do something fun together. He's not doing that today, so I give it a try.

"Hey, Dad, want to walk Toby around the lake?"

"No thanks, Cleo," he says, staring at a blog on his computer.

"How about a bike ride?"

"No thanks."

"Maybe we should go someplace where you could meet a new girlfriend!" I suggest, though I don't know where that would be.

Dad laughs a little bit. "That's easier said than done," he says. "Cleo, this may be tough for you to understand, but it's really, really hard to find someone who you really love."

"Love?" I'm shocked. "You *loved* Terri?"

"Yep, I did. I do," he says.

I roll a chair over next to his computer and sit down by him. "I mean, I know she was more than a girl-who's-a-friend," I say, "but I just thought you liked her a whole lot."

"No, Cleo. There was a lot more to it than that."

"Like what?"

Dad turns away from his computer and looks at me. "Well, I didn't tell you this before because I didn't want you to know how serious I was about her, but she's part of the reason we moved to California."

"What?" I ask. I had no idea Dad kept secrets like this

from me. I thought we told each other everything . . . but when I think about the voodoo doll, I know that's not true at all.

"I met her two years ago, at a conference she came to in Ohio. We talked a lot, and she came back to visit a couple of times. . . ."

"Where was I?" I ask.

"Usually at Jane Anne's house for the weekend," he says, and I can't believe Dad was living this whole other life without me. "But I knew Terri and I couldn't get closer unless we lived in the same city. I liked the sound of California and a fresh start. I didn't really have any reason to stay in Ohio, Cleo. It had been ten years since your mom passed away. That's a long time to live in the same house with someone who's not there anymore. I talked to your uncle Arnie about it a lot. . . ."

I can't help but interrupt. "You talked to Uncle Arnie about all this?"

"Well, he and I don't have a lot in common, but he understood how I needed a change. We also knew it would be hard for you, here in a new place and not knowing many people at first. That's probably why he sent you that ridiculous doll for your birthday."

That's a topic I do *not* want to discuss, but I don't have to because Dad continues. "Anyway, after I met Terri, Uncle Arnie turned out to be a good person to talk to."

"You could have talked to me!" I say. "I'm always here!"

Dad laughs. He pulls my chair closer and puts his arm around me. "I know you are, Cleo. But this was grown-up stuff. So when I decided that you and I could both handle it, we moved. And I do think the change was good for you."

He's right. The change *was* good—at first. Even though some kids like Madison were mean, Samantha and I became best friends. Now I'm thinking it might have been better if we stayed in Ohio, where I didn't have any friends to lose and Dad only had girls-who-were-friends.

"In all the years since your mom, Cleo, I never met anyone I thought I could love as much. Your mom would always say there was a special magic that brought us together. And I never felt that magic after her, for all those years."

"Until Terri?" I ask, but I already know the answer.

"Yep, until Terri. She was different. Is different. I was waiting for you to love her too. Then I was going to ask her to marry me."

"Marry you?" I ask. Wow. Dad has a lot of secrets, just like me. "If you and Terri had gotten married, does that mean she would have been my mom?"

Dad shakes his head. "No one else can be your mom, Cleo. But Terri would have been a very good friend."

"A friend would be good right now," I say. He pats me on the shoulder and goes back to reading the thing on his computer—or pretending to.

I text Samantha a couple of times and tell her I want to

talk. What I don't say is that I've made a really big decision and she's not going to like it at all.

Sam has made most of the decisions up until now, and I've gone along with her ideas. Now it's my turn.

I've decided I need to get the doll back from her and destroy it once and for all.

The problem is . . . well, there are a lot of problems. I have no idea how to get the doll back, and I don't even know if it *can* be destroyed. According to Scabby Larry and Albert Einstein, matter doesn't go away; it becomes something else—like snow becomes water or Marty the millipede became plant food in the ground. What if I get the doll back, and I throw it away or burn it or give it to Toby to play with, but it still has its power? There'd always be the danger that something could go wrong again, no matter how good someone's intentions might be. And now that I really think about it, Sam's and my intentions weren't always good. We just pretended they were.

There's only one person who has the answer to my questions. I call Uncle Arnie. But when his computer screen comes on, no one's there—just Fuzzer, his cat, sitting on the desk licking his paw.

"Uncle Arnie?" I ask, wondering where he is.

"I'm a cat now, Lil' Cleo!" Uncle Arnie's voice booms. "A crazy N'awlins voodoo queen put a hex on me, and I became my own cat!"

"Oh no!" Boy, Sam and I have caused a lot of trouble, but at least we didn't turn anyone into an animal. "What are you going to do?"

Right when I realize Uncle Arnie is joking, his face joins his cat on-screen. "Sorry, Cleo, didn't mean to scare you! I was just kidding around. But you shouldn't joke with voodoo. I know that for a fact." He holds up his hand with the icky scar that he says came from a stove. "See, that was an important lesson for me. If you don't take voodoo seriously, people can get hurt."

"I think I already learned that lesson, Uncle Arnie." He must see how upset I am because he asks what's wrong. I don't want to tell him everything, so I just say that the doll has started to spook me and I think I should get rid of it.

"Well, that's too bad, Cleo, because Positive Happy Voodoo Doll is only meant for good, as you know. But now that you've got me mulling it over, I suppose there's always a chance things might go wrong. Some of the more crafty and conniving people down here in New Orleans, I could see them finding a way to take a good thing like this and make bad things happen. Though I guess it could happen by accident too."

Now he tells me.

"That's why I try to spread positive happy juju," Uncle Arnie says. "There are enough bad things in the world already."

I can't disagree with him there either. I'm not proud that

I had anything to do with bad, mean juju, mojo, gris-gris, or hoodoo—accidentally or on purpose—and that's why it's time to end it.

"So . . . how do I destroy it? For good?"

Uncle Arnie settles into his chair, and I can tell he's taking this seriously. "Well, Cleo, I designed my dolls to work best with two people so kids could learn about the power of togetherness and friendship instead of being alone. I hope that's worked for you."

It's too complicated to explain how it did and then it didn't, so I just nod.

"The same principle applies to destroying the doll," he says. "First off, you and a friend need to rip it in half." He picks up a doll that kind of looks like mine and attempts to rip it. He pulls on its arms and nothing happens. His face gets red as he pulls one arm and the opposite leg. He grunts and tries one more time, but the doll doesn't rip.

"See, Cleo, this is why you need a friend. It's hard to do yourself. But I'm sure you and your pal will be able to do it together." He tosses the voodoo doll offscreen, and it must hit something because there's a loud clanging sound. The cat meows and looks up lazily. "Once it's ripped in half, you can use scissors to cut it into smaller and smaller pieces. Then you need to bury it in two separate places—one near you, and one near your friend. And that's it."

I'm quiet as I let it sink in.

"Sound like you can do it?" he asks.

"I'll try," I say. "Thanks, Uncle Arnie. And don't turn into a cat."

He holds the cat in front of his face. "I'll try not to, Cleo!" And then he and Fuzzer are gone.

Now I have my answer, but I still have a problem. Sam is my only friend, and she's not going to destroy the doll with me; that's for sure. I can't tell Dad about any of this, and I don't think he'd count as a friend anyway. There isn't anyone else.

Or is there?

24

On Monday I'm in Kevin's classroom before Samantha. When she comes in, she doesn't even look at me. I wonder what her weekend was like—if it was as sad and depressing as mine.

In Focus! class, she sits on the other side of the room, next to Scabby Larry. Normally she doesn't even go near him. And in Recreational Wellness, as we play field hockey inside the gym on the wooden floor, she cracks her hockey stick on the ground loudly whenever she's near me.

I stay late after school for *Healthyland* callbacks. I should have taken more time over the weekend to learn the script, but I spent almost all my time thinking about Uncle Arnie's advice instead, and I came to a decision. It's going to be hard to do, but I'm going to do it—today. Sometime. Eventually.

"Okay, everyone! Welcome to callbacks! This is going to

be fun, so get ready!" says Roberta. "Let's start with everyone sitting on the floor in a circle around me."

We all move to find a place, and Madison ends up next
to me. She quietly says hi and I say hi back; then Roberta
starts our first exercise. She says we're going to tell a story,
but she can stop us anytime, right in the middle of a sentence, and someone else will have to keep talking in the
exact spot the person left off. Roberta tells us that the story
is going to be about a baby called Happy Baby meeting a
dog called Downward Dog. She points at Larry, which means
he's the one who starts. "Once upon a time, there was a
Happy Baby who lived in Healthyland," he says, totally confident. "His parents took him out for a walk, but he crawled
away and ended up in a doghouse." He looks to Roberta, but
she makes a hand motion for him to keep going. Now I'm
worried she's going to point at me, but excited too. Larry
continues, "Happy Baby looked at the walls—"

Roberta points at Madison, and Madison immediately
says, "And wondered why this dark little house smelled like
his diaper." We all laugh at that. "Happy Baby decided to
crawl out of the house, but—"

Roberta points at me. My mind goes blank for a minute;
then I say, "But all of a sudden, a big furry creature was in
the doorway. This was Downward Dog, and he said, 'What
are you doing in here, smelling up my home?'" Everyone
laughs at that too, in a good way, and I tell a little bit more

of the story until Roberta points at someone else and I can breathe easy.

When the game is over, Roberta says we'll now perform the sections of the play that she gave us before. She says she knows this could make some people nervous, so we'll do our performing one at a time, with just her. The rest of us can sit out in the courtyard and practice or do homework. She calls the first person to audition and the rest of us leave the room.

Outside, Madison sits at a picnic table. It looks like she might be reading her script, but I know that if I don't talk to her now, I may never get the courage.

This is it. Madison is the decision I made over the weekend. I realized that all of our positive voodoo started to go wrong when we made it about her. We were pretending our hexes were positive things, but really, they were negative. And even if Sam and I stop, I feel like the negativity will still be out there unless she knows what happened. That's when I decided I needed to tell Madison everything. Whether she believes it or not. Whether she hates me or not.

I walk over, and of course I stumble on a rock before I get to the table. She looks up but doesn't make a face or say anything.

"Are you studying your part?" I ask.

"I guess so," she says. "But I practiced a lot over the weekend so I'm probably ready."

"You're getting a part for sure. You'll probably be the lead."

"Thanks," she says. "You'll probably get a funny part."

Right away I think she's making fun of me. "Why?" I ask.

"You're good at improvisation. You say funny things during the exercises."

"Oh. Thanks, I guess."

"So. How are things with you and Samantha?" Madison asks.

Since that's a really hard question to answer completely, I don't say anything right away.

"I'm sorry," she says. "Maybe that's personal."

"No," I tell her. "It's actually something I really want to talk about. If that's okay."

Madison looks like she didn't expect that, but says, "Sure, I guess." I sit down and face her across the picnic table. I warn her that I have a story that's going to sound as wild and wacky as anything that might happen in Healthyland. And that she's probably going to call me crazy by the time the story is over, but it's all going to be true, every bit of it, from the time the package arrived at my house to this past Friday, when Samantha decided she wasn't my friend anymore.

Madison says she'll keep an open mind. She says she reads a lot of science fiction and fantasy books, so she's used to fantastical stories. Now it's my turn to be surprised. I never pictured Madison reading books that are popular with nerds and dorks . . . and people like me.

"Okay," I say. "If you like that stuff, get ready. This is going to be a weird one."

I expect her to stop me, to get up and leave the table, as soon as I tell her about opening the box and finding the voodoo doll. Instead, she seems intrigued and says, "Cool." I expect her to be mad when I tell her how Samantha and I decided to make ourselves popular by hexing her, but she's not. Instead she says, "So that's why you pulled my hair out!"

"Yes!" I say, maybe too enthusiastically. I calm myself down. "I'm sorry about that."

Madison doesn't seem to care. "So, wait a second. What exactly did you do when you . . . hexed me?"

"Well, the first one—" I start to say, but she cuts me off.

"There was more than one?"

"There were . . . two," I say, looking down and mumbling.

"Two?" She sounds shocked.

I look up and nod. I'm beginning to think that telling Madison wasn't such a great idea.

"So what did you do?" she asks. She doesn't sound mad, just interested.

"Well, for the first one, we thought one way for us to get popular was for you to embarrass yourself, like, beyond belief, so—"

"Oh my gosh!" she interrupts again. "Focus! class! The day I . . ."

"Farted. Yeah," I say. "That was us."

"Well, that was definitely embarrassing." She looks to the side like she's thinking about something. A second later she says, "But you know, that could've been a coincidence."

"You farted like a mule on the exact day we wanted to embarrass you and it was a coincidence?" I ask. "That's pretty hard to believe."

"Harder to believe than a voodoo doll that really works?" she asks. I shrug. What do I understand about the world anymore? Nothing. But Madison seems to be putting some pieces together in her head. "I'm pretty sure that was burrito day—the day that happened. My mom says I should work at a gas station because I'm so gassy when I eat certain foods. We never eat beans at home anymore."

I nod, but I feel like I'm in a dreamland. Madison Paddington with her long golden hair is telling me, through her perfect pink puffy lips, that she gets gassy.

"So what was the second one?" she asks.

"That one was worse, Madison. That's the one I feel really bad about. But we didn't know what was going to happen. We just wanted you to be nicer. We had no idea what would happen next. And it wasn't what we expected—at all." I take a breath. I know I'm going to have a hard time saying it. But Madison saves me the trouble.

"Ohhhh," she sighs. "The day I went crazy."

"Yeah," I say, hoping she hears the "sorry" in my voice. "We only wanted you to get nicer. We didn't want you to get suspended or get your parents so mad at you. . . ." I stop myself from saying more. I don't want to talk about her parents. "But that's what's wrong with voodoo. It doesn't turn out like you think it will!"

Madison looks lost in thought. She's probably going to let me have it now. Maybe she'll even use a few of the curses she used that day. And I'd deserve every single one of them.

"I don't know, Cleo. That could have been a coincidence too."

"What?" I shout. "But you never acted like that before! I mean, you'd say mean and snotty things to me, but never . . . that!"

"Well, you're right—in a way. I never had been exactly like that before. But you know, I've been going to a therapist once a week since I was eight. You have one, right?"

I think therapists are the people I've seen on TV, the ones who listen to your problems and try to help you solve them. I shake my head.

"Oh, maybe you'll get one later," Madison says. "My therapist, Kimberly . . ."

Of course she would only have a first name.

"She believes I have some anger in me, deep underneath the surface, and that on that day, it all came out."

"What could you be angry about?" I ask. "You're perfect!"

Madison almost snorts when she laughs—just like Samantha and I do. Or did. "Now that's funny! No, the perfect one is my sister, Bronwyn. She's in high school, and she's never done anything wrong in the whole history of the world. I'm not as good at cheerleading, I'm not as good at acting, and I read science fiction books instead of magazines about how to put on makeup or meet a boy. In a way, I didn't even mind cursing and messing up that big and that bad. My parents know I'm different from Bronwyn now! I was sick of always trying to be perfect for them anyway."

"But you didn't mess up," I say. "Samantha and I did. Especially me."

"Or maybe you didn't."

"That's really nice of you to say, Madison, but I just can't believe that both of those hexes were coincidences."

"Well, if they weren't—and they worked—why does Samantha hate you now?"

Of course this is another long story. I explain how Sam and I wanted her mom and my dad to get together so we could be sisters, and how we wanted *good* things to keep Terri away from my dad, but she ended up in a car accident. Madison looks sad when I tell her about how my dad and Terri broke up. I can't believe she even cares. She doesn't know Dad *or* Terri. She barely knows me.

"So what happens next?" Madison asks.

"Well, here's where it gets really hard," I say. "You think the hexes weren't real, and I kinda think they were. Either way, I don't want the doll making any more trouble."

"Why don't you get rid of it then?" asks Madison.

So I explain how Samantha has the doll and I need to get it back and destroy it with a friend. "I know we're not really friends," I tell her, "but you're the only person I could think of."

Before she answers, Roberta shouts, "Madison Paddington!"

Madison picks up her script and her backpack and stands up. But before she walks away, she says, "I'll do it. Let's talk tomorrow."

I watch as she practically skips toward Roberta. I sit by myself and think about how strange the world has become since that weird little doll showed up in my life. My only friend became my enemy, and my enemy has heard our entire story, and not only does she understand it, she even wants to help me solve my problem.

It's all so strange and surprising, I barely even remember performing my audition. But Roberta calls me later that night and tells me I got a part. I'll be playing a tree, but that's not as bad as it sounds. Tree is a yoga pose, and this tree even has a few lines.

25

The rest of the week passes slowly. Madison and I text sometimes, but we only talk at play rehearsal since Samantha isn't involved. Finally it's the weekend, but at home when the doorbell rings, I don't run and slide to get there. I just walk down the hallway like a normal person, though what Madison and I are going to do today is about the farthest from normal I can imagine.

By the time I get to the front door, Dad has already opened it. And there stands Madison Paddington. She's as pretty and perfect as when she was the most popular girl in school, but she's different now. And so am I.

I see Dad talking to her in the doorway and hope he doesn't say anything embarrassing. "Hi, are you Madison?" he asks. She says yes, and he asks, "Are you by yourself?" He's looking around for a mom or dad.

"My nanny dropped me off," she tells him. "My parents both had appointments today."

I know what that means. They had more important things to do.

I don't want Dad quizzing her anymore, so I jump in between them. "Hi, Madison, want to come to my room?"

"Sure," she says, and Dad lets her through. "Thanks for having me over for this playdate, Mr. Nelson."

That surprises me. "You call these playdates?" I ask. "Sam told me playdates were for little kids."

"I wouldn't know," says Madison. "I've never really had one."

"What do you mean? I thought you'd have playdates all the time. You've got Kylie Mae and Lisa Lee and everyone else."

"Too busy," Madison says. "Too much on my schedule. I'm lucky I got to come over today, but I told Sonia, my nanny, that I finished all my homework. She wanted to go shopping anyway, so she didn't mind getting rid of me."

It's sad to me that everyone wants to get rid of Madison. Dad seems happy to have me around most of the time, even when I drive him nuts.

I close the door once we're in my room. Right away she notices my terrarium and sees Millie crawling across a piece of bark. Madison gasps and jumps back a little bit.

"Oh, sorry," I say. "I should have warned you."

"That's okay," she says. "As long as he stays in there."

"He won't go anywhere, I promise."

"He's actually kind of cute," she says, taking a closer peek at him. "Just not in my hair!"

Wow. Madison is not turning out to be who I expected . . . at all. When she looks around the rest of my room, she sees my drawings and my robots and my monster dolls, and she seems to like them too.

"I'll show you everything another time," I say, then wonder if there ever *will* be another time. Once we solve this problem, will Madison Paddington come to my house again? *Maybe,* I think, since she looks pretty comfortable right now, sitting right on the floor, not worrying about dog hair or dust or anything. She even pets Toby, who is coming dangerously close to drooling on her designer skirt and short, shiny high-heeled boots.

"So I have a plan," I tell her. "I just want to see if you agree first." She nods and I hit her with it.

(1) We tell Dad that Samantha has texted us and wants us to come to her house. (2) Dad drops us off at Sam's, and we convince Sam's mom that Sam invited us over. (3) We ambush Sam and demand the doll back. If she doesn't give it to us, we'll ransack her room. (4) We retrieve the doll. (5) We call Dad to get us. 6) We destroy the doll following Uncle Arnie's instructions.

It's very easy to list these things. But I tell Madison they're going to be very hard to do.

"Then we'd better get going," she says, giving Toby a pat on the head and standing up. I shout "Dad!" and we get started.

Dad grumbles about driving us to Sam's, but I tell him it will be good for him to go outside and get some fresh air. Since Terri broke up with him, he doesn't do anything but work. The house is getting messy again and Toby fur is piling up like a carpet on sections of our floor. I suggested once that we make chicken and rice and bacon green beans for dinner, but he only wants to make frozen dinners or order in food.

"I know what you can do!" I tell Dad. "You don't even have to come up to Sam's. I know how to get there. You should drop us off and go to that coffeehouse you like so much, and treat yourself to an iced Americano with soy milk and half a sugar."

Dad laughs. He asks if this would be okay with Madison's parents, and she says it's fine as long as she's back here in time for the nanny to pick her up.

So Dad drives. I encourage him to listen to music instead of a podcast. I don't want to *tell* him to cheer up because that would never work, so I'm hoping to do it through little suggestions like iced Americanos and music on the radio.

When we get to Sam's condo building, Dad stops the car and says, "I really should walk you two up there."

Madison jumps right in. "Oh, Sam's mom doesn't want

to be disturbed. She's, um . . . getting a massage. Sam's text said that we should go in quietly and go right to her room."

I'm impressed with Madison's quick thinking, and I build on it, like we learned with improvisation. "Yeah, Dad, she wouldn't have time to talk to you anyway."

"Well, that's *fine*." The way Dad says it lets me know once and for all that he doesn't like Sam's mom, at least not in a girlfriend way. He says he'll wait and watch us go in the building, and we should call or text him in an hour so he can pick us up.

"Thank you, Mr. Nelson," Madison says as she gets out of the car.

"Yeah, thanks, Dad," I say, remembering to be polite. Then I slam the door with a smile that probably shows too much of my teeth.

I know the code to open the front door of Sam's building, so that part's easy. As Madison and I get into the elevator, I see Dad's car pull away. I feel like I did when I tried out for *Healthyland*—nervous, but excited. But the worst thing that could've happened at that audition was embarrassment— and I'm used to that. This could be dangerous if Sam's mom realizes we're up to something!

"That was a good one, about the massage," I tell Madison.

"Thanks. My mom gets them twice a week so it was easy to come up with."

The door of the elevator opens and we're on Samantha's

floor. Madison follows me to her door, and we both take a breath before I knock. This is it.

Sam's mom opens the door. She's in a fancy sweat suit like she wore with my dad, but this one is lavender instead of pink. I wonder if she's going on a hike with another girl's dad, but I don't ask. I just say, "Hi! Sam told me and our friend Madison that we could come over for a little bit."

Paige looks uncertain but lets us in. "Samantha didn't tell me this," she says. "Have you two made up?"

"Sort of," I lie, or rather, *improvise.* "We're trying. That's why we came over."

"Well, good," her mom says. "We miss you and your dad."

At the mention of Dad, I shoot Madison a look. *See,* the look says, *she loves him.* Madison gets it. "Well, we'll go back to Sam's room then," I say, and walk ahead. We don't want Sam's mom seeing her reaction when we ambush her.

"Okay. I'll be down at the pool if you girls need anything." She picks up a beach bag and a big floppy hat, and heads out the door.

Perfect. She'll be out of the house for what's going to happen next.

I slowly turn the doorknob to Sam's room and open the door. Sam's voice booms, "Mom! I told you to knock!"

I open the door all the way and Sam sees us: her best friend (until recently) and her archenemy standing together in her doorway. Now she yells "Mom!" in a different way. She *wants* her mom now.

Madison and I step inside. "Your mom's at the pool," I say.

"What do you guys want?" Sam asks. "What are you even doing together?"

"Cleo's my friend," Madison says. Sam looks as shocked as I feel hearing that. "She told me everything. We're taking the doll back so nobody can do any more hexing."

I can tell everything that's going through Sam's head: she can't believe Madison is my friend, she can't believe I told her everything, and she definitely can't believe that we're here to take the voodoo doll.

"It's not here," she says, acting tough. She takes a few steps backward toward her dresser, where her phone is sitting.

"Grab her phone!" I order Madison, and she does. It feels good to be in charge of a plan for once! "You're not gonna call your mom," I tell Sam. "You're going into your closet and getting the doll out of its hiding place."

"What hiding place?" Sam asks innocently.

"The one you told me about. In the back under all your old toys."

"Oh, *riiiiight,*" Sam says, nodding. "I forgot about that." I can tell by the smirk on her face that her mind is churning. I just don't know what she's thinking.

A second later, Sam says, "Okay, you got me. I'll be right

back, *once I get the doll.*" She turns slowly and walks into her closet. Madison raises an eyebrow at me with a look that says, *This is going to be easy.*

But I suddenly know Madison is wrong. I close the door to Sam's closet with a loud slam. "Hand me the chair from her desk!" I shout, and Madison does it with lightning speed. I jam the chair underneath the closet's doorknob and hope that it keeps the door closed like in movies and TV shows.

"Cleo!" Sam shouts from the other side of the door. "What are you doing? I have the doll!"

"No you don't! I thought it was in there, but you never would have given it up that fast. I know where the doll is and I'm going to get him!"

Madison doesn't know what's going on, but I don't have time to explain. The closet doorknob is shaking and the door is making noise on its hinges.

"Don't worry, Sam," I shout. "We'll be back real soon!"

"Back?" Madison asks. "Where are we going?"

"I'll tell you on the way," I say. Samantha is shouting the whole time—she's going to tell her mother; we're going to get in trouble; I'm never going to have another friend again. But I don't care about any of it; I've got a job to do.

The banging of the closet door is getting louder. I don't know if Sam will be able to get out, but I know we should hurry either way. "Follow me!" I shout to Madison as I climb through Sam's bedroom window.

Madison is right behind me—through the window, into the condo's outdoor hallway, down the steps, and onto the sidewalk. We run for a block. I'm wearing sneakers so it's pretty easy for me, but Madison's high-heeled boots slow her down. When we get to the corner, we both stop, breathing heavy. "Crab soccer hasn't trained me for this," Madison says, pinching her waist and bending over. I have to laugh. She's right!

Instead of running down the next block, we just walk quickly—until I throw my arm out to stop Madison. "What's wrong?" she asks.

"My dad!" I whisper, but it sounds like a shout.

We're almost in front of Caffeine Craze—the exact coffeehouse where I told Dad to go! There's a big window looking out onto the street, with tables and umbrellas outside where people are enjoying their iced Americanos or whatever their special order is.

"My dad is in there!" I explain urgently. "What if he sees us?"

I think about running to the other side of the street, but there aren't any stop signs or traffic lights, so that seems like a bad idea. When I turn back around, Madison isn't there. She's on her hands and knees on the sidewalk, crawling past the tables and umbrellas and coffee drinkers, right under the front window. She doesn't even care about her skirt getting dirty or her knees getting scraped. I get down and follow her, so we're just two girls crawling on a sidewalk in the middle of Los Angeles. Not something you see every day.

We get past the window and stand up. I can't help myself, though; I have to peek inside. I only allow my forehead and one eyeball to lean in—and I see Dad at the counter, stirring sugar into his coffee. I pull my face away a millisecond before he turns around. "Run!" I shout to Madison, and we both take off down the road.

I'm antsy waiting at the stoplight. I look behind me to see if Samantha is following us, but luckily there's no sign of her. Madison and I take off as soon as the light changes, and I lead her to the entrance of the graveyard. She stops at the gate, huffing, puffing, and pinching her side again. "The doll's here?" she asks. When I nod, she says, "This place is big. How are we going to find it?"

"Oh, I know where it is—sort of." Even though I'm tired, I've got the energy to keep running. I know Madison is following because I can hear the clicking of her boots on the paved path. I'm not sure exactly where Samantha and I turned onto the grass, but I make a guess and take a hard right. A second later, Madison yells, "Poop!"

I turn around. Madison's on the ground. I can't help laughing because she said "poop" instead of a curse word— since I know she can yell every one in the dictionary and a bunch that aren't! "Are you okay?" I ask, running back to her. She's facedown in a pile of soft, thick dirt. She pushes herself up and I see black smudges on her hands, her clothes, and her knees. She sits up, not upset at all, and starts pulling off her boots.

"I'm fine," she says. "My heel got stuck in the dirt and made me fall over." She puts both boots on the dirt and says, "Let's go."

"You're gonna leave them here?" I ask. They probably cost as much as all my shoes put together!

"We'll come back and get 'em. The guy under here isn't gonna want them." When Madison says that, I realize she didn't just fall down in some dirt; she fell on a new grave!

I can't help squealing. "Ewww, there's a dead person under there?"

"There are dead people under everything," Madison says, totally matter of fact. She's standing up now. "Okay, where are we going?"

"Follow me!" I say, and I start running. I'm not completely sure I'm going in the right direction; I'm just hoping for the best. It was pretty dark when Sam and I were here before, and the place looks different in the bright sunshine. Whenever we pass a flat gravestone, I read the name. I see a Dillenbeck, a Gerber, then a Rupelmyer and a Neff.

"Where are you *going*?" Madison shouts from behind me.

Right then I stop. I've almost run right on top of him. Harold Rocap.

"The doll is around here somewhere," I say.

We split up and look around. I peer up into the big tree with the witchy-finger branches, but I don't see any box or doll. Madison's picking up flower arrangements on the gravestones nearby and looking underneath. It's really lucky that she's not scared of dead people! I walk a bigger circle around Harold's stone, and then I see something unusual: a small square of fresh dirt. Not big enough to be a grave like where Madison fell, but the right size for a voodoo doll.

"I think this is it!" I shout. She runs over, and without even talking we get down on our knees and start digging with our hands. Madison, who probably gets weekly manicures like her mom, is plunging her hands into this dark, soft dirt and totally ruining her fingernails!

It doesn't take long to hit something. I'm praying I'm right and that it's the voodoo doll and not a skull or a bone or a murder weapon or something even scarier. "There's something here!" Madison says.

After a few more handfuls of dirt, I see him. The doll's face is looking up at us, dirtier than ever before, but with the same stitched smile, same button eyes, same yarn hair.

"Wow!" Madison says. She seems impressed, which is pretty unexpected considering what this little doll did to her.

I pick him up out of the ground. "Let's go," I say. We stand up and turn toward the paved path, but something— or someone—is in our way.

26

Samantha leans over us.

Her hair is standing up like a crazed clown's wig and her face is as red as a crazed clown's nose. But this clown is also a thief—holding up a pair of short high-heeled boots that aren't hers.

"How . . . about . . . a . . . trade?" It takes her a long time to finish because she takes a breath in between each word.

I look at Madison.

"No trade," Madison says, and starts walking away. Slowly. Coolly.

"Madison's got plenty of shoes and those won't fit you anyway, Sam," I say. "So why don't you just hand them over?"

"Only if you give me the doll! Come on, it's *ours*!" Sam shouts, trying to grab it from under my arm. I hold it tight and start to run.

"It's mine, and it won't be *anyone's* soon!" I yell, running.

Suddenly I feel something hit me in the back—not hard, but enough to make me turn around. I look down, and there's one of Madison's boots on the ground. "You're throwing a boot at me?" I shout as the other one comes flying at my face. I duck out of the way.

"You really didn't think that through, Sam!" I say as I pick up both boots and run, catching up to Madison.

I feel bad that she has bare feet but there's nothing I can do besides hand over her boots. We make it through the gate and to the corner with the traffic light, where we have to stand and wait. And wait. The light across from us is red, but by looking at the green light in the other direction, I can see how long we have until it changes. Inside a square box on the traffic pole, a red hand is flashing and numbers are counting down. It's the slowest counting I've ever seen. 10, 9, 8 . . .

I move my weight from one foot to the other, bouncing nervously. Not talking. Just looking at the countdown, then looking behind us. That's when I notice Madison has plopped herself down on the ground and is putting on one of her boots. Though this light is taking forever to change, I don't know if she has time for *that*! 7, 6, 5 . . .

I see Sam in the distance, and she's getting closer.

When 2 flashes, I take a step off the curb. Madison stands up, one boot on, the other in her hand. Finally the countdown gets to 1, and then we have to wait even longer for the light to turn green. Then we run.

As we're crossing the big road, I hear Madison scream, "Ow!" I turn, hoping she hasn't fallen down. She hasn't, but she's avoiding putting weight on her bare foot. Oh no. Maybe she stepped on something sharp. "What is it?" I ask when she meets me on the corner.

She lifts up her foot. "Just a rock," she says, picking it off her foot and throwing it on the ground. "Let's go."

We run some more, Madison bobbing up and down like a creature in a horror movie because of her one boot. When we get halfway down the block, I turn and see Samantha stuck at the traffic light. Good. That flashing red hand will keep her waiting awhile.

A few minutes later, we see the coffeehouse umbrellas in the middle of the block. I stop Madison from running so I can look at the people at the tables. Luckily no one has Dad's messy black-and-gray hair, which is easy to spot. We both take a breath. Madison sits on the curb to put on her other boot while I put the doll safely in my backpack and zip it up tightly.

I'm sweaty and tired but I try to slow down my breathing before I walk into the coffeehouse. I see Dad's head right away. He's looking down reading a newspaper, wearing his thick round glasses and holding a big plastic cup half filled with ice and coffee.

I wish he were here with Terri instead of alone.

"Hey, Dad."

He definitely wasn't expecting to see me. "Cleo! What are you doing here?"

I have to think fast. "Ummm . . ."

So much for thinking fast.

"Ummm . . . ," I continue. Then I come up with something. "Oh! Samantha's mom went down to the pool, and Samantha wanted to go too, but since Madison and I didn't have anything to wear, we decided to come get you and go home."

"Where's Madison?" Dad asks, looking behind me.

"Oh . . . she saw a friend of hers, one of the kids sitting outside, so she's saying hi." I glance through the window, and of course Madison is nowhere nearby.

"Would you two like a drink?" he asks, putting down his paper. "Iced tea? Juice? Smoothie?"

A strawberry-blueberry-banana smoothie would be awesome right now, especially after all the running, but I know better. I want to get out of this coffeehouse and into Dad's car. "Nope, nope, nope, I don't want anything, and I'm sure Madison doesn't either. Let's go and have water at home. Lots of water!" I tug at Dad's T-shirt sleeve. "Come on, let's go."

He takes his time getting to his feet. First he has to fold his newspaper, then he takes off his glasses and puts them in their case, then he grabs his big messenger bag to put it over his shoulder, and I'm just thinking, *Come on, come on, come on.*

"Madison, what happened to you?" Dad asks.

I turn around, and Madison is standing there looking like a totally different girl from the one Dad met at our front door. Her hair is as messy as mine, her cheeks are red, and there are patches of dirt from her neck to her knees.

"Oh, nothing. We were, um, playing in the dirt by Samantha's house."

I can't imagine many reasons for three eleven-year-old girls to play in the dirt, and I'm sure Dad can't either, so he looks confused. "You guys crammed a lot of fun into such a short time. Are you done talking to your friend, Madison?"

Madison has no idea what he's talking about, but since she's excellent at improvisation, she just says, "Yeah." Then she looks at me like, *What?*

I'll explain it all to her later. Right now we've got to get out of here. We walk toward the front door, and when Dad pushes it open, there's someone in his way.

Samantha.

She's redder than Madison and breathing heavy.

"Samantha! I thought you were at the pool," says Dad, walking through the door and onto the street. Madison and I stay close to him.

"Whaaaa?" she asks, but she can't even pronounce the *t* because she's wheezing like someone who really needs an inhaler.

"What's wrong?" Dad asks. "Are you okay?"

"No!" she manages to spit out. "I'm not! I had to chase Cleo and Madison. . . ."

"Chase them? Why?" Dad asks.

Madison and I look at each other. Will Sam really tell my dad what just happened? How could she? There's way too much to tell and it's way too unbelievable.

Samantha breathes a few more times. "Um, I had to chase them because I had Cleo's doll, but I . . ."

She buried it in a graveyard! Is she going to share *that* with my dad?

"What exactly is going on here?" It sounds like Dad is getting irritated. This is not going well.

Madison jumps to the rescue. "It's all part of a game we were playing, Mr. Nelson."

It doesn't look like Dad believes her. He turns to Samantha. "So this was just a game, Sam?"

Usually Samantha has everything figured out; she's thought everything through way in advance. But not now. The look on her face is telling me she's stumped. It's the first time I've ever seen her this way. She has no idea what she could tell my dad that would make any sense.

"Yeah," Sam finally says. "We were sort of, um, playing tag in the neighborhood."

Dad looks at the three of us one by one. So far he's been told that we've been playing in the dirt, we turned down going in a pool, and now we're frolicking on the city streets playing tag.

"Cleo, is this true?"

"Yeah," I say. "I didn't want to tell you because I knew you wouldn't want me to leave Sam's house without permission. But her mom lets her."

Dad is skeptical. "I don't know," he says. "Maybe I should call Sam's mom and see what's up." He opens his big bag and starts rooting around for his phone.

"No, Mr. Nelson, it's fine. I'll be home in one minute and thirty seconds. You can time me. See you!"

And Sam takes off down the street, her sneakers pounding the sidewalk loudly, her curly hair bouncing up and down.

Dad closes his bag and looks down at me and Madison.

"I don't know what went on today, girls, but I'm sure I don't like it."

I look at Madison; then I look up at Dad. Finally I say something truthful to him, maybe for the first time all day.

"We won't do it again."

Dad must have enjoyed reading the newspaper at the coffeehouse because he doesn't make a scene or yell at me in front of Madison; he just sighs. On the way home he asks us if any of this storytelling and running around had anything to do with boys. Madison and I squeal "ewww" and "gross" and "ick," so he knows we mean it.

"Well, that's a relief," he says, and turns up the radio.

Back at the house, Madison and I go to my room. As soon as we close the door, we both fall to the ground laughing, groaning, and letting out all the stress our bodies have felt all day.

"What now?" Madison asks.

"We have to get rid of my little pal."

I unzip my backpack and pull out the doll. I hold him in my hand and look down at him. Aside from the wine and dirt, the smell of cinnamon, and the leftover oatmeal mix, he's not that different after all of this. But I sure am.

I look in the doll's scratched button eyes and silently say I'm sorry for what has to happen next. But it's what Uncle Arnie said we had to do.

I find some music on the computer and crank it up loud. I grab the voodoo doll's legs, Madison takes hold of his arms, and we pull in opposite directions. He doesn't rip at first, so we say, "One, two, three!" and yank even harder. It works. He tears in two and his insides fall to the ground, making a giant mess on the floor. It looks like corn and birdseed and kitty litter and the wood chips from the bottom of the guinea pig cages at Pets! Pets! Pets! There's some fuzz too—stuffing or dryer lint, I can't tell.

I notice something bigger—I don't know what—sticking out of a clump of fuzz. I get down on the ground and sift through the mess to pick it out.

"What is it?" Madison asks.

"A . . . heart," I tell her.

Between my fingers is a wooden heart, the size of a big marble and just as smooth.

"What's that for?" Madison asks.

I hand her the heart. "I have no idea."

Madison looks at both sides, then makes a discovery. The heart opens into a locket, with a place for a picture in both sides. "Cleo, look at this," she says, lifting a little slip of folded paper out of the middle and peeling it open. "It looks like a note. Maybe it's for you?"

She hands it to me. I open it, wondering what the heart of this voodoo doll could possibly have to say to me. Maybe it just says "Made in China" or something.

"Well?" Madison asks.

First I read it to myself. Then I read it again. It definitely wasn't made in China. It was made by Uncle Arnie.

"It says 'Friendship is the meeting of love and magic.'"

I can tell Madison likes the sound of that. "I think that's true," she says.

We're both quiet for a few seconds; then Madison speaks up again. "So, is it time for the scissors?"

I look at the heart in Madison's hand, the piece of paper in mine, the chunks of tan material and yarn, and the mess on the floor, and I say, "I think so."

I hand her my scissors and she starts snipping her half of the doll into pieces. I use my hands to rip apart the bottom half. It's not easy, but I've got extra energy from the running and the music and the fact that it's all over. Madison, cutting the hair off the doll's head, says it's adrenaline.

I put my half of the pieces on my desk. Madison does the

same with the yarn and buttons and material she cut. We mix it all together, and then Madison scoops up half and puts it in the outside pocket of her backpack. She'll bury it somewhere near her house, far away from the other pieces—which I'll put in the backyard next to Marty. Maybe I'll write *magic* in stones by this grave.

Toby barks and scratches at the door. When I let him in, he immediately starts licking up the mess on the floor. "No, Toby!" I shout. I grab him by the collar and drag him back into the hall. He can come in again after I've cleaned up—whenever that is.

27

Things get back to normal at school after that. Well, as normal as things can be after everything that happened. Sam and I don't become friends again, but we're not enemies either. I'm not mean to her and she's not mean to me. We just don't talk much except to say hi. As far as I know, she never told anyone about our voodoo adventure.

I was a little afraid that Madison would get bored with me after we solved our voodoo problem, but we actually become better friends. We sit together at lunch, sometimes with other people from the play. When we're waiting to practice our *Healthyland* scenes, she tells me about the latest science fiction book she's reading and I make her laugh by drawing pictures of the characters she describes. We go to each other's houses to hang out on the weekends. Hers is big and glamorous with way more rooms than her family needs. I like it there because we can practice Spanish with her nanny, but I don't like the healthy snacks she has to eat. I teach her Pig Mania and explain how Terri introduced us to the game but hasn't come back for it since she broke up with Dad. Madison and I also talk a lot about how I want Terri and Dad to get back together. I want to figure out a way, and Madison wants to help, but we're having a hard time because they're grown-ups. Their lives are different from ours. Plus, we don't know much about love and romance. But we're always thinking.

At rehearsal one day, I ask Madison's opinion on inviting Terri to the play. She says it's a great idea, so that night I sit at my desk in my pajamas, with Toby at my feet and Millie by my side in his terrarium. I know it should be an easy text to write, but I don't know exactly what to say.

Hi Terri, this is Cleo. Remember me? I decide that sounds dumb. Delete.

Hi Terri, I've been thinking a lot about you lately. Too serious. Delete.

Hi Terri, I'm sorry I didn't write before but I hope you might still be my friend. At that moment, Dad sticks his head in my room. Delete, delete, delete!

"Okay if I come in?" he asks. "It's almost time for bed."

"Yeah, I was just finishing up something," I say, tossing down my phone and jumping into my sheets.

"Wow, I've never seen you go to bed that quickly," Dad says, laughing. He's about to turn off my light, but I stop him. There's been something on my mind for a long time now, ever since I told Madison about our hexes. And after trying to write that text tonight, I decide this is the time.

"Dad, can I tell you something?"

"Of course, kiddo."

"You might want to sit down."

"Oh," Dad says, still sounding jokey. "It's something serious!" He sits at the bottom of my bed, and I guess when he sees my face he realizes I really *am* serious. His voice changes. "What is it, Cleo?"

I gulp. I take a breath. I gulp again. It's time.

"Remember that voodoo doll Uncle Arnie sent me?"

"Yeah. I haven't seen it lately," he says, looking around my room.

"I got rid of it," I say. "It was doing bad things." I think about that, and though it's hard, I say the truth. "*I* was doing bad things."

Dad doesn't laugh or say I'm being silly, and I'm glad. "Like what?" he asks.

I decide to skip what happened to Madison and go right to the things Dad would understand. "Well, one time Samantha and I cast a spell, and Toby got skunked the next day," I tell him. "I mean, we didn't hex Toby to get skunked—we were trying to do something good for ourselves, but we made a mistake and used his hair. So you had to lock him in the laundry room, which kept you two apart."

Now he does laugh, but I know he's not being mean.

"Well, first of all, I told you not to play with that voodoo doll."

"I know. I'm sorry." And I really am.

"But second of all, it's not real, Cleo. Dogs get skunked all the time in this neighborhood. And it'll probably happen again to Toby, God forbid, even with no voodoo doll around."

"I knew you were going to say that," I tell him. "But the other one is much worse."

"What else did you do?" he asks, and I can tell he's not expecting anything more serious than the dog smelling bad for a day.

"Terri's car accident . . . ," I start to say, but I can't finish. My throat is closing up and I'm feeling tears in my eyes.

"Oh, honey," Dad says. He slides up closer to me and puts his arm around my shoulder. "Don't tell me you think you caused Terri's accident."

"I did!" I say. I'm crying, which I hate—*don't like*—but I can't help it. Then I let it all out. "Sam and I wanted to be sisters and we thought if you liked her mom you might get married, so we wanted you and Terri to be apart. And now you are! I'm sorry, Dad. I'm sorry I'm sorry I'm sorry!" I have to turn away from him and put my head in my pillow because I'm crying so hard.

Dad spends a couple of minutes rubbing my back and saying, "Cleo" and "Honey" and "It's okay." But it's not.

When I get tired and quiet down, he tells me to turn around.

"Cleo, there are lots of reasons Terri and I are apart right now. Our problems were there before your voodoo doll ever showed up at our house. And maybe she and I will work it out someday, but I don't want you ever—*ever*—to think it was your fault."

"But—" I say. He stops me.

"A car accident can happen to anyone. And my breakup with Terri was not your fault either. Not in any way whatsoever. You have to tell me that you hear me. That you understand."

"But—" I say again.

"Butts are for cigarettes," he says.

I smile a little. "Butts are for panda bears," I tell him.

"Butts are for rhinoceroses," he says.

"You know what butts aren't for?" I ask.

"What?"

"Millipedes!"

"You're right!" He laughs and stands up from my bed. "Do you feel a little better now?"

"A little," I say.

"You'll remember everything I said, right?"

"Yeah, I guess."

"Don't guess. None of this was your fault. Okay?"

I'm not sure I completely believe him, but I still say, "Okay."

He turns off my light and closes the door. I wait until I hear his footsteps far down the hallway. Then I sneak out of bed and grab my phone. I hear the sound of the TV in the living room, so I know Dad won't discover me. Once I pull up my messages, I type my text.

Hi Terri. I hope you're feeling better. And I hope you'll come see my play this Friday night at 7:00 p.m. at Friendship Community School. I'm a tree, but it's really better than it sounds. Love, your friend, Cleo

That's good enough.

28

Three weeks after the Great Destruction of the Voodoo Doll (as Madison and I call it), it's the opening night of *Healthyland.* It's actually the only night of *Healthyland,* but "opening night" sounds more glamorous.

Backstage, the adrenaline is running inside everyone. And though we're supposed to stay backstage, I can't help peeking through the curtain to look at the people getting settled into the rows of folding chairs. Madison's parents are both looking at their phones, not talking to each other, but at least they're there. It's easy to spot Dad, of course, even though he's looking down and reading something in his lap. I can't blame him for reading, though; he has no one to sit with. A few rows behind him, on the opposite side of the auditorium, I see Sam and her mom. That's interesting. When I said hello to Sam at school today, she didn't mention she was coming.

Roberta shouts, "Places, please!" and I take one last look around the auditorium. I'm glad I do, because I see some red hair moving in the back row. Terri must have just walked in! There's no bandage on her face, but it looks like she has a cast on her wrist. She didn't write back to my text, but I'm so glad she got it. Seeing her makes me even more excited to be The Tree tonight!

It's hard to describe the show. It's almost like a dream. I remember laughing with people (quietly) as they came backstage after playing their parts. I sort of remember being onstage and saying my five lines:

"I am the mighty, leafy guardian of the forest."

"I give shade, I give oxygen, and," I said, raising my arms, "I grow and grow."

"Like rock and mountain, I will not move."

When we were rehearsing, I didn't understand that line, because trees *can* move sometimes. So Roberta let me add two other lines that I wrote myself. "I will not move . . . unless I fall down in a storm or tornado or someone cuts me down and takes me somewhere. Then I might become a porch or a tree fort."

It's fun to hear people laugh at that. And when I run off-stage, Madison gives me a hug, then Larry does, and Roberta too. Other kids pat me on the shoulder or say "Good job."

The show feels like it goes by way faster than the hour it really takes to perform. At the end, we all go onstage together and bow in a long line. The lights in my eyes are too bright to see individual people, but I can hear the applause and see that the audience is standing.

Afterward we go into the auditorium lobby, where there are cookies and lemonade for everyone. Before Madison goes over to her parents, she nudges me, points toward my dad, and says, "Uh-oh." He's talking to Sam and her mom. "You'd better go break that up."

I say goodbye to Madison and walk over to Dad, Sam, and Paige. They stop talking when I get there.

"Hey," says Sam.

"Hey," I say back.

And that's it. A moment later, Samantha's mom interrupts this great conversation. "Sam, honey, I'm going to head out to the car. Come out when you're done talking to Cleo, okay?" Sam nods.

"I'm going to get a lemonade. Okay, Cleo?" asks Dad. I nod.

Now it's just me and Sam. I realize I haven't had a real talk with her in weeks.

"You did a good job," she says, looking at the floor more than she looks at me.

"Thanks. Did your mom make you come?"

"No. I wanted to. I wanted to see how you did. And, you know, see Madison and Scabby Larry and everybody."

"We just call him Larry," I tell her. "He's really fun when you get to know him better."

"Oh, okay," Sam says. Then it's quiet for a second. "So you had a good time?"

"Yeah!" I say. "You should try out for the next one!"

"Really?"

"For sure," I tell her. "You feel really dopey sometimes, like when you try out and even during practice, but you get to hang out with people you normally wouldn't hang out with and it's really exciting when you perform! You definitely should try out next time!"

Samantha doesn't exactly smile, but her lips turn up a little bit at the edges. "I'll think about it." We stand there for a second with nothing to say. Sam shuffles her feet a little, then says, "You never told me what you did with the doll."

"Oh, it's gone. Ripped up and buried."

Sam sighs. "Well, that's good, I guess."

"Yeah, I think so too."

"We used to have fun doing other things besides . . . that, didn't we?"

"We did," I say. And I guess I've known it ever since she got mad at me, but right now, I miss Sam. I hope someday we can be friends again.

It's quiet again for a moment. Sam looks around the room and then points toward the lemonade table. "Hey. Check it out."

I look over and see Dad—talking to Terri.

"I'd better go say hi," I say to Sam.

She nods. "I'd better get to the car. See you Monday."

"Yeah, see you Monday," I say, and I'm so excited by everything that's happened today, I give her a hug. When I look at her face afterward, I can tell she didn't expect it, but I don't care because this is a great night!

I look over toward the lemonade table again, and I wonder what I should do. I don't want to interrupt them if they're busy falling back in love, but I can't stand here alone in the middle of the activity either. Then Terri makes the choice for me. She spots me and shouts, "Hey, it's the star of the show!" I run over and hug her, making extra-sure to be careful of her wrist. She holds her lemonade away from her so it doesn't spill on us and tells me I did a great job.

"Thanks for coming!" I say loudly. "Dad, did you know Terri was here?"

"Not until I saw her out here." He thanks her for coming too, but he says it in a soft, sweet way. I'm hoping they'll hug or even (yucch) kiss, but instead she says, "I should go. Invite me to the next one, Cleo."

"I will, Terri, for sure!"

"Bye, Bradley. Nice to see you," she says, and touches him on the back. It's not a hug or a kiss, but at least it's a start.

"Nice to see you too," he says, and we both watch her walk away for a minute. Then Dad turns to me, looking happy. "So, what do you say? Ice cream at home?"

"And some TV?" I ask.

"Hey, it's Friday, and it's your big night. We can watch whatever you want!"

"Maybe past midnight?"

"Don't push it," he says jokingly. But I know I'll be able to stay up as late as I want.

When we get home, there's a gift waiting for me. Dad and I open the front door and Toby greets us in his usual barky, slobbery way, but tied to his collar is a bunch of helium balloons. They're shiny and colorful and some of them say *Congratulations*. Hanging underneath Toby's chin is a small envelope with my name on it, tied to a ribbon.

I sit on the floor, open the envelope, and read the card inside.

Sorry I couldn't be there tonight, Cleo, but your dad's going to send me a video. I know you are a star—and a tree! Congratulations! I hope it was a splendiferous night.

Love & magic, Uncle Arnie

I don't know why, but my heart feels big and full. I look up at Dad and ask, "How did Uncle Arnie get balloons on Toby?"

Dad laughs. "He ordered them, and I put them on Toby."

"Oh," I say, though inside I'm thinking, *Duh.*

Just like Dad promised, we scoop out big bowls of ice cream. We don't have to eat the crusty vanilla-chocolate combination that was already in the freezer, because while I was at school, he went to the store and bought my favorites— rocky road and cookie dough. We watch lots of TV, and though I'm still excited from the play and seeing Terri and the balloons and the ice cream, I start getting tired. But I don't want this great day to end, so I ask if we can watch some more. Dad nicely says no; it's bedtime.

I take my balloons to my bedroom and tie them to a knob on my dresser. There are so many and they're so festive, I decide to untie one from the rest of the group and give it to Dad. I pick a silver one that has a confetti design on it and head down the hallway in my pj's. "Dad, I have a present for you," I say.

Dad is sitting at his desk and turns around. He smiles when he sees the balloon and thanks me for sharing. "I'm glad you came back out; I remembered that Uncle Arnie sent you something else, and he asked me to wait until after the play to give it to you."

He hands me a cardboard box that probably came special delivery, just like the voodoo doll. It isn't voodoo-size, though; it's a lot smaller, like for a piece of jewelry. But I know Uncle Arnie would never buy me jewelry.

I plop myself on the floor of the dining room and ask Dad to hand me a pair of scissors so I can open the box. It's stuffed with newspaper, but instead of throwing it to

the ground like I did with the voodoo doll, I take my time
and look through it carefully. That's when I see what he's
sent. It's a little red glass bottle, small enough to tie a string
around and wear as a necklace. There's some liquid inside.
I pop off the lid and take a sniff. It doesn't smell bad; it
doesn't smell good; it doesn't smell like anything.

Just like with the voodoo doll, there's a note at the bottom of the box. The paper is light purple with pink roses
around the edges, and Uncle Arnie has attempted to write
in pretty cursive handwriting.

*The time for voodoo is over. Now it's
time for the magic of love!
When you're ready, this love potion
will improve your life and the lives of
others. Instructions to follow.*

Love & magic, Uncle Arnie

"What is it?" Dad asks.

I hold up the bottle and show him. But after everything
I've told him about my voodoo, Dad's not ready to hear
about a love potion. I'm not sure I'm ready for it either. "Just
a little perfume," I say.

"Finally, something normal," Dad says, then adds that
it's really time for bed now. Though I'm getting too old for
it, I let him walk me to my room and tuck me in.

"I'm proud of you, Cleo," Dad says.

"Really? Why?" I ask.

"This has been a hard couple of months, but you've handled it really well. I can tell things are going to get better and better for you."

Maybe he's just saying all that because it's my big night, but I still like hearing it. I hope I can live up to what he feels about me. We'll see.

I must start to fall asleep against his shoulder, because when he moves I kind of wake up. "Good night, Cleo," he says.

As he leaves the room, I say, "Thanks, Dad. This was a weird day, but it's the best day I've had in a long, long time."

"Me too, honey." He turns off the light and closes the door, so it's just me and the darkness.

Alone in bed, I can't fall asleep. I have too many things going through my head. My mind is so full of ideas. All kinds of ideas. Voodoo didn't turn out the way I expected, that's for sure. No matter what Dad and Madison say, I don't think I'll ever be sure the doll didn't work. Everything happened: the pizza treat for Sam, us being popular (even if it was only for a short time), Madison becoming nice, and Terri being apart from Dad. And I can accept all of those things—except that last one.

That's why my brain is about to jump out of my head right now. A voodoo doll—even a Positive Happy Voodoo Doll—is one thing, but a love potion is something totally different. Now I know how things can go wrong, and I wouldn't let that happen again. And though I don't care about love that much, I care about Dad. And I care about Dad and Terri.

I know Uncle Arnie's gifts have gotten me into trouble before, but what I'm thinking about wouldn't be trouble; it would be love. I find my phone on the floor and text Madison.

Got a plan for Dad and Terri. You in?

A minute later, my phone dings with a text.

Of course! is Madison's response.

Cool. See ya Monday! I write.

She writes back: ☺

I lie back on my pillow and look up. I don't know what's going to happen next, I don't know what school is going to be like from day to day, and I don't know if I'll be able to get Dad and Terri back together. But I have my friends and my family and my dog and my millipede. I have love and maybe some magic, and right now, that's all I need.

Acknowledgments

An author writes alone, but the final product is definitely a group effort. Many thanks to my agent, Jennifer Rofé, who put me through my paces, and my editor, Caroline Abbey, for seeing potential in Cleo. You've made my childhood dream come true.

Others who loved Cleo right off the bat were the young people who read early drafts and gave me great input: Sarah Geithmann, Niko Parker, Henry Dorosin, and the Darkrai Book Club: Emerson Herrera, Ethan Hsu, Brandon Hsu, Miles Straw, and Eoin Janeiro.

Adults were helpful too, of course. Thanks to LA's Writing Pad, where Cleo spoke her first words, and to my early readers Monte Smith, Lamar Damon, Steve Grieger, Kimberly Gerber-Gallagher, and my brother, Kenny Gallagher, who will *not* be getting paid $10 for his efforts.

No stranger to storytelling, TONI GALLAGHER earned a journalism degree from Northwestern University and has a successful career in reality TV. She began as a story editor on the early seasons of MTV's *The Real World* and was a producer on the beloved Disney Channel show *Bug Juice*, about real kids at summer camp. Currently she is executive producer of *The Real Housewives of Beverly Hills* on Bravo. Toni lives in Los Angeles and loves finding the magic in it. Visit her at tonigallagherink.com.